HEART AND SOUL
POEMS by

CAROLYN GRASSI

Carolyn Grassi's collection of poems charts a personal and spiritual autobiography in plain language that sings and is deeply resonant and moving.   *John Ashbery*

These poems tell a vital story--the struggle between a religious calling and the love of life. In poetry full of wonderful details of her Catholic childhood we follow the poet into the convent, into her forbidden love for a priest, into an intricate and compelling love drama and the struggle between devotion and desire. Desire, it turns out, opens her way into a more personal devotion outside the convent. *Naomi Ruth Lowinsky*

Carolyn Grassi's *Heart and Soul* is fascinating in its fluent and affecting blend of memoir and poetry, reminiscence and sheer invention, loss, grief and homage. Adopting a persona at times, or imitating a seminal influence on her writing at other junctures, she has created a quilt of memories and reflections on a life's education--the journey we all hope to make from becoming to being, or from acting as disciples to representing ourselves and our art as apostles.   *Ron Hansen*

ALSO BY CAROLYN GRASSI

BROOKLYN BEGINNINGS POEMS
(Patmos Press, 2021)

TRANSPARENCIES, POEMS
(Patmos Press, 2004, 2022)

JOURNEY TO CHARTRES, POEMS
(Black Swan Books, 1989)

MARY MAGDALENE
AND THE WOMEN IN JESUS' LIFE
co-authored with Joseph A. Grassi
(Sheed and Ward, 1986)

HEART
AND
SOUL

POEMS by
CAROLYN GRASSI

Foreword by Ron Hansen

Patmos Press
San Francisco, California

Patmos Press
San Francisco, California

Available at:
local Bookstores or Amazon

Cover painting:
"Wisdom and Innocence" by Johanna Baruch
http://johannabaruch.com

Cover designed & arranged by
zip2print.com
San Jose, California

ISBN 978-0-9742435-1-1
Library Catalog Card Number 2013909381

FOREWORD BY RON HANSEN

Carolyn Grassi's *Heart and Soul* is fascinating in its fluent and affecting blend of memoir and poetry, reminiscence and sheer invention, loss, grief and homage. Adopting a persona at times, or imitating a seminal influence on her writing at other junctures, she has created a quilt of memories and reflections on a life's education--the journey we all hope to make from becoming to being, or from acting as disciples to representing ourselves and our art as apostles.

The girl who confessed her sins at Holy Cross Church, in the Flatbush neighborhood of Brooklyn, who taught city kids to swim in Silver Lake at Camp Oh-Neh-Tah, who yearningly played Elvis tunes on her trumpet as she dreamed of a boy, surprises us by entering the Maryknoll Novitiate in Topsfield, Massachusetts: "*No TV, radio, newspapers or phone use. Only / visits from family twice a year. Letters / limited to once a week, none during Lent / and Advent.*" The life is hard enough that it is fitting that the formidable Mistress of Novices "*loomed in my mind as a Marine / sergeant might for recruits,*" and yet Carolyn discovers that Sister Paul Miriam was "*a passionate / nature lover, a fine painter and possessed / an adventurous spirit . . .*"

She likens that cloister experience to the fretful friendship between Gerard Manley Hopkins and Robert Bridges, to the passionate but impossible love of Søren Kierkegaard for his Regina, to the self-abnegation of Thérèse of Lisieux, the enclosure and pining of Saint Clare for Francis of Assisi. And she's aware of what "*on the other hand*" she sees in a Jesuit theologian, a specialist on the sacrament of marriage, who one Easter leaves his religious order and his university job because, finally, *"Love is making a personal appeal. Indecision's a thorn / in your side."*

A sequence of poems describes the potent effect that the tortured fifteenth century Spanish mystic Juan de la Cruz has on Teresa of Avila, whom Carolyn imagines seeking his spiritual direction and living some of his *Dark Night of the Soul.* And she surprises us again with a giant leap in years and locale to California, now a mother of two sons and married to a former priest.

The fraught conditions of friendship float through the poems focusing in the next remarkable sequence on Wordsworth and Coleridge, the former famous, though for me the more minor poet, and hovered over by the three women in his house, while Coleridge is lonely, rejected, and seemingly a failure in the estimation of the literary world, yet secretly pined for by Wordsworth's sister Dorothy.

And there are more intriguing poems in this soulful collection: a fairy tale version of the Annunciation that has been praised by John Ashbery, miniature meditations on Donatello's bas-relief of Christ in the Victoria & Albert Museum, travel sketches from Milan, Versailles, and Mont San Michel, and a poignant poem set in California's Point Reyes seashore in which she imagines her late mother present. That poem ends with the hymn *"Come, Holy Spirit,"* an image evoked in the flight of a heron across the Bay.

Joseph Grassi, Carolyn's husband, and my Scripture professor in the nineties, declined in health and finally passed away while some of these poems were being composed, and his gentle, genial presence is felt in her memories and revisions--in particular in the moving closing section *"Sanctuary."*

Carolyn's religious faith animates nearly all the poems in this collection. She's said of her work that "*I wish for readers to feel, whatever struggles they go through in life, the Source of our being shall never abandon us on the journey.*" That Source is very present here. Written informally, in an intimate, conversational style, it nevertheless is a book full of wisdom, substance, sensual attentiveness and, yes, *heart and soul.*

————

Ron Hansen's novels include *Desperadoes, The Assassination of Jesse James by the Coward Robert Ford, Mariette in Ecstasy, Exiles, Atticus*, a finalist for the National Book Award, and his most recent book: *She Loves Me Not: New and Selected Stories.*

Death happens, love happens in everyone . . .
If one loves what is frail and mortal, if one loves
Holds on . . . must not one's love become changed?
There is only one absolute imperative,
The imperative to love . . .
                    Iris Murdoch

. . . it is only by first trying to restore the past
That one comes to discover one's future path.
                    W.H. Auden

All art is an act of confession.
                    James Baldwin

The manuscript which reposed
Above her heart began shuffling
And beating, as if it were a living thing . . .
                    Virginia Woolf

I

BROOKLYN AND THE CATSKILLS

"... the earthly Paradise is the state of innocence,
  the whole journey   . . .   is thus a return journey in
search of the true starting place--   the return to original
    innocence."
        Commentary by translator Dorothy Sayers of
            Dante's *Purgatorio, Canto XXVIII*

" .   .   .   rivers and life have always seemed to belong
  to one another.   The wonder of bright water with
overarching shadows hit me when I was so small that
I had to reach up towards my father's hand   .   .   ."
      Freya Stark, *The Minaret of Djam,*
              An Excursion in Afghanistan

LEAVING BROOKLYN BY FERRY

Grandma Skea called her father *"a seafaring man,"* since
he captained ships for the Cunard Line in Liverpool,

and sailed on the ship taking Stanley to Africa. Dad's
grandfather sailed a schooner to the South Sea Islands.

My brothers and I paged through his photos of pristine
beaches, men carving boats, kids climbing palm trees,

women with orchids in their dark hair, homes on stilts,
wild capped waves. Pacific Islands, a world away from

Brooklyn, though fortunately Dad frequently drove us to
Owl's Head Park facing New York's harbor. We kids

climbed trees, spotting ocean liners filling Hudson Bay.
Horns blasting. Fireboats spraying rainbows. The first

in our family to sail was Aunt Muriel, who welcomed us
into her cabin aboard the Queen Mary. At the 67th Street

pier, we kids ran to catch heavy wet ropes tossed from
tug boats to loop over steel pier posts. Captains waved

us aboard, down narrow silvery stairs into a pirate-like
cave. Copper engines glowing. Pistons, pumps hissing,

humming. Drum roll of motors underneath our feet.
Swaying, bouncing, nearly off-balance, as the boat

rose and fell, rubber fender bumping against the dock.
Boys shouting as they jumped off posts into oil slick

waters. Cars rumbling over steel ramps of the ferry to
Staten Island. Skyscrapers reflecting a New Jersey sunset.

Heading home, I'd kneel on the back seat of our car for
a last look at the portholes like Christmas lights of big

ships on dark night waters. Grandma sang *"By yon bonnie
banks and by yon bonnie braes, when the sun shines bright*

on Loch Lomond. " Dad longed to own a boat, so sail in
Jamaica Bay. He never sailed, never left Brooklyn, except

the subway ride under the East River to work in the city,
drives to Long Island's Jones beach, Sunken Meadow State

park, or across the Brooklyn Bridge to the Bronx Zoo and
Museum of Natural History. Unforgettable our crossing

the George Washington Bridge. Palisades cliffs glowing
in the Hudson below our car as Dad drove to his boss's

home in the woods of Smoke Rise, New Jersey. A private
lake with sailboats. Twice we went there as guests. Years

later, after Dad died, my brother John sailed as a Naval
officer to Vietnam; his son Paul enjoyed boating on

Georgia's lakes. Brother Richie and wife Loretta raised
their family in New York's Seven Lakes region. Many

times Joe, I, Eddie and Peter crossed over Golden Gate
Bridge, rode the Tiburon ferry to Angel Island, sighting

Alcatraz, the Bay Bridge, Berkeley hills, San Francisco
skyscrapers, Sausalito marina's sparkling sailboats.

3

MRS. HANLEY, PROSPECT PARK
in memory of Mrs. Mary Hanley

Mrs. Hanley pushes baby Jackie's carriage
    as little Francis rides its rim. Seven kids
tag along, including me and my best friend,
    Judy, the oldest of Mrs. Hanley's children.
On leaving Lott Street, we turn left at Albemarle
    Road, then a right onto Bedford Avenue for
ten blocks till seeing the gates of Prospect Park
    at the Kings Highway entrance, while singing
camp songs along the way, rounding the path
    past the sprinklers pool, struggling up hill,
down a slope into a lush green meadow ringed
    by maples and elms. Judy, Barbara, Jane
and I hold tight to a sheet we toss high letting
    it fall slowly as a puffy parachute, then we
shimmy up a maple tree, whose twigs, leaves
    and branches scratch and tickle our arms
and legs. "*Look! There's the city across the river.*"
    Mrs. Hanley calls from the meadow: "*Time
for lunch!*" Reaching deep into the carriage,
    she pulls out a big paper bag overflowing
with peanut butter & jelly sandwiches, chips
    and a thermos of lemonade. No four-leaf
clovers today, but a single shining buttercup
    I lift under Mrs. Hanley's chin. "*Look Judy,
your Mom loves butter.*" A small yellow circle
    shimmers on her fair Irish skin. She's rocking
baby Jackie, as we gather round singing her
    favorite lullaby: "*Tura Lura Lura, Tura Lura Li . . .*"

HOLY CROSS CHURCH, FLATBUSH, BROOKLYN

Our darkly lit church resembles a cave, where a handsome
    angel stands in the sanctuary by the tomb as he touches
his lips, signaling for silence, while we start singing

"Alleluia! Christ has risen," Holy Dove flies across
    the ceiling, where Saint Helen sits upright in a bed,
as she opens her arms to welcome the *"holy cross."*

I daydream during Mass, until classmate Aileen
    whispers and makes me laugh, then a serious nun
taps the pew and says: *"Both of you meet me after Mass."*

So, there we are in a convent dining room. Aileen sitting
    across from me at a long table. Sister angrily says:
"I want you both to pray the Act of Contrition out loud."

I wonder if I'll remember all the words? Aileen begins:
    "I confess to Almighty God and to the Blessed Virgin Mary
and to all the saints that I have sinned exceedingly in thought,

word and deed . . ." She smiles through her fingers, that
    she shapes into a church steeple, then waves wildly,
when Sister turns her back, while I'm mumbling through

the prayer. Many times, Natalie and I laugh in church,
    especially on Saturdays, when she exits Father
Donnelly's confessional, getting caught in the heavy

drape that pulls on her shoulders, while I smile from
    Father Kiernan's line. I like his gentle voice as he
treats my *sins* of answering back my mother, of cursing,

or fighting with my brothers as venial offenses,
    easily erased by absolution, three *Hail Mary's* at
the altar rail, where I meet Natalie praying her penance.

Soon we're pushing through double doors at the back of
    the church. Laughing as usual, though Natalie's face
reddens when she talks about Father Donnelly: *"Cookie,*

my heart beats so fast when I go to confession or for spiritual
    direction." *"Oh gee!"* I say, thinking of the handsome,
young, Irish-American Fathers Donnelly and Kiernan,

who oversee our Friday night parish dances; only my heart
    never beats fast for either priest, though it does for
Jimmy Morris, praying he will ask me to dance to *Elvis,*

Fats Domino, Little Richard, the Platters or a *Buddy Holly*
    song filling our parish auditorium, or better yet a slow
dance to *"Good Night Sweetheart"* before Father Kiernan

ends the evening singing *"Danny Boy."* Aileen doesn't
    go to parish dances. She's going steady with Billy.
I picture them *necking* during a movie in the balcony of

the RKO Kenmore on Church Avenue at the corner of
    Flatbush Avenue. Natalie and I head to Henry's Ice-
cream parlor on Nostrand Avenue, packed with teenagers.

Sipping a vanilla egg cream, I'm pretending not to look,
    as I look, for Jimmy. Natalie's enjoying a root beer
float. We walk to her apartment. I take the bus home

to Newkirk Avenue, run three blocks to our East 26th
    Street apartment. Before entering the convent, Natalie
switches spiritual directors, so takes two buses to reach her

confessor in Canarsie, an elderly serious priest, who had
    no clue about *"Rock and Roll."* Natalie never mentioned
Father Donnelly again; neither did her face get red. After

several years in the convent, she marries an Italian guy,
    who loves opera. During my novitiate, Joan Burke,
a Holy Cross classmate, writes to say Aileen died at age

eighteen. She doesn't know the cause. Soon after leaving
    the convent, I marry an Italian-American former
priest, gentle as Father Kiernan. When we move west,

I lose touch with friends back east. Via an internet search
    I locate Natalie's brother. He responds to my email:
*"I'm sorry to say Natalie died several years ago. I'll mail you
her rosary, since were best friends. She'd want you to have it."*

SILVER LAKE, CAMP OH-NEH-TAH

At age ten, I started going every summer to
    Camp Oh-Neh-Tah in the Catskills, singing
with other city girls in the meadow as we went
    to and from the dining room overlooking Silver
Lake-- *"Morning comes early and bright with dew,
    under your window I sing to you, up then with
singing, up then with singing, let us be greeting
    the morn so new."* White birches, silvery aspens
thick pine groves glistening along the shore. Mists
    rose over the far lagoon, giant turtles winging
through murky waters. My swimming lessons
    began in *The Crib*, a slippery wooden pool,
where leeches loomed below, so I avoided standing,
    while working hard to pass the Beginners test,
so swim in the deep waters of *The Bucket*. After
    a few summers, I became a counselor and taught
swimming to girls from New York's inner city.

Many feared the lake. *"Pretend you're in a bathtub.*
Take a big breath, put your face under. Blow bubbles.
    Stretch your arms. Point your toes. Push off and
glide into my arms." Scary and fun for Barbara,
        Arlene, Julie and I practicing our water ballet
set to a John Phillip Sousa record, while Miss Jackie
        directed: *"Tumble head over heels off the dock,*
keep time to the beat, lift your arms, kick your legs,
    arch your backs, now go under pulling backwards."
Holding tightly with my feet to Barbara's shoulders,
    she pulled us down into dark waters as I prayed
she'd reach the surface soon. Unforgettable August
    hurricane tearing through camp for over a week.
My cheerful postcard home: *"Hi Mom and Dad,*
    It's so exciting! The lake's getting higher. Our locker
room's overflowing, so we wear boots in the dining hall."
    Once the storm subsided, campers and counselors
rowed to the middle of the lake at twilight, Miss Dot
        leading songs: Flocks of birds flying into the forest.
Sun setting over Hunter mountain. Always ending
        the evening with *"Day is done. Gone the sun from*
the lake, from the hills, from trees. All is well. Safely rest.
    God is nigh and goodnight." Rowing to the boathouse,
following a flashlight trail. Owls hooting. Bats zipping.
    Mosquitoes buzzing. Girls giggling. At age eighteen
I'd enter a convent overlooking the Hudson. No more
    swimming, boating or singing *Taps* under the stars.

HOMESICK

"When I was a camper at Oh-Neh-Tah
    I lived by the side of the lake, klonk! klonk!
I listened to all the lovely noises the little
    bull froggies would make-- klonk! klonk!
Chatter wong wong.   Chatter wong wong.

Chatter Da Dee. They sang by the side
of the lake-- klonk! klonk!" Aileen and I
    learning the song as the bus headed
north on the thruway. Ten-year-old girls
    on our way to the Herald Tribune Fresh
Air camp in the Catskills. Kids coming
    from Hell's Kitchen, Harlem, the Bronx,
Red Hook, Canarsie, Flatbush, Bedford
    Stuyvesant and other city neighborhoods.
Unforgettable my first overnight in our
    camp meadow. Miss Mary pointing with
a flashlight at planets and stars, whose names
    sounded wonderfully mysterious. I fell
asleep gazing at Venus and Saturn, not waking
    till Miss Jackie's trumpet blasts at dawn
and shockingly cold mists swirling round
    my face. Crawling out of the damp sleeping-
bag, Aileen and I hunted for twigs to help
    start the breakfast fires. Miss Sally let us
strike the matches to light the tinder. Aileen
    stirred a large pot of thick oatmeal. I jabbed
a plastic spoon into a small cardboard box
    of *Raisin Bran.* Sitting silently on a boulder
overlooking Silver Lake, the nearby forest
    reminding me of the Flatbush tree lot,
where Dad, Richie, John and I picked a pine,
    carrying it home on Christmas Eve, sweet
pungent sap sticking to my mittens. Mom
    waiting with lights, bulbs, tinsel and a big
silver star for the top. Crushed pine needles
    on the carpet, perfuming all our apartment.

WINDHAM HIGH PEAK

Thrilled to be returning at age twelve to
    Camp Oh-Neh-Tah in the Catskills of
East Windham, New York. Daydreaming
    beside the open window of Papago cabin
during rest-hour. Pines, aspens, birches,
    elms, oaks, and maples filling the nearby
forest of Windham High Peak, the mountain
    I longed to climb since I was ten years old.
At last I was going with a small group along
    with Miss Sally and Miss Mary singing--
"I love to go a wandering along the mountain
    trail and as I go I love to sing my knapsack
on my back. Valerie, Valera, Valerie, Valera
    hahahaha . . . my knapsack on my back."
We were taught how to make trail markers
    with a hatchet. *"Strike gently at a slant.*
Never cut deeply. Stand safely back. Mark both
    sides of the tree showing the way up and
down." After slicing a strip of shiny birch,
    I stuffed it in my pocket. (Once home,
I'd write in blue ink on its papery surface--
    "Windham High Peak"). Sweating, climbing,
briefly resting, finally we settled on a high ledge
    over-looking the valley. Cool breezes round
my bare legs. Hawks gliding past my face. Bees
    buzzing in nearby berry bushes as we ate
sandwiches. Aileen played with a bright orange
    salamander she found sunbathing on top of
a gray boulder. I felt drawn to Silver Lake aglow
    as a jewel set beside the dark green forest.

SUNDAY AT CAMP OH-NEH-TAH

At dawn on Sundays someone woke me,
	since they saw the sock I tied to the railing
at the foot of my bed, meaning I was *a Catholic*
	and needed to get to Mass. I ran through
the cool misty meadow with a few other girls
	to a yellow bus we rode to a small country
church in East Windham. Miss Mary was
	the only counselor aboard. Most campers
and counselors were Baptist. In early evening
	we sang *Vespers,* the *Doxology* and gospel
hymns before a crackling fire and finally at
	the end of two weeks, we swayed as one
family at the council fire as Miss Dot bowed
	and rose to the north, south, east, west
directions, white smoke curled in the dark sky
	as she prayed to ancient spirits of the forest.

CABIN INSPECTION

Not everything about camp was happy-go-
	lucky. I dreaded cabin inspection by Miss
Hazel every morning. She checked each corner
	and cranny, rubbing her fingers along
the ledges and under our beds for tiny dust
	balls. She checked to see if *the hospital
corners* were properly made. Any wrinkle
	in a blanket meant a minus point against
the cabin. Our tops, shorts, socks, underwear,
	and towels must be folded so their smooth
side faced towards the cupboard door. After
	lunch the scores for each cabin were posted
on the Nature Hut. Demerits were clearly
	described, so everyone knew under whose
bed a dust ball was discovered, if clothes

11

were out of order or other housekeeping
mistakes. At a formal ceremony she awarded
      ribbons to the girls whose cabin received
the highest score. No cabin I was in won
      a yellow ribbon for neatness. I received
a blue one for swimming, a red for archery,
      green ribbon for climbing Hunter Mountain.
Being neat and orderly was never my talent,
      though I tried my best for the sake of our
cabin's score. Neither did I excel at orderliness
      in the convent. A frequent reprimand by
sister superior was: *"Why haven't you reported
      about your messy closet?"* Keeping tabs on
infractions was not something I took seriously,
      though I knew she did. A few words of
encouragement, as ribbons of approval, might
      or might not have made a difference in my
overall performance at neatness. I imagined
      God approved of my attempts at singing
Gregorian chant and how with Sister Marianne
      we balanced our weekly Hanover bank deposits
for the priests wing of our Order. Not a child
      hearing my name called at a camp ceremony
for learning to shoot a bow and arrow; instead
      chapel bells for Holy Saturday's night fire,
reminding me of ceremonial camp fires, when
      I danced and chanted to Spirits of the forest.

THE LATRINE

Away from home for the first time, the scariest
      thing was in the middle of the night, if I
needed to take a pee, so, flashlight in hand,
      I'd follow the forest trail over the foot bridge,
then climb the wooden stairs of the large latrine;
      once inside, I ducked down far as possible,

afraid of being attacked by flying beetles or hit
        by huge moths that circled the bare light bulbs.
Scary, too, sitting on the open, non-flush toilet,
        worrying if strange creatures lurked below
in the dark. I'd rush back to the cabin, jump
        into bed, burrowing within my blanket. Next
summer, at age eleven, I'll be bigger, braver.

TRUMPET LESSONS

Carrying my school books and trumpet under
        my arms, I rode the Flatbush Avenue bus
to St. Joseph's High School's ten story building
        (once headquarters for the phone company)
on Bridge Street to downtown Brooklyn with
        old, young and middle age passengers of
various ethnicities, typical of our borough, bouncing,
        lurching, swerving, since the bus stopped every
few blocks, passing Merkel's Meat Market,
        Hunt's Fish Store, Macy's, the Lowe's Kings,
Fanny Farmer's, Sears, Thom McAn's, Dale Green
        Dance Studio, Erasmus Hall High School,
the Dutch Reformed Church, RKO Kenmore
        Theater, Bickford's, then the bus picked up
speed alongside the maple trees dividing Prospect
        Park and the Botanical Gardens, swinging
round Grand Army Plaza's peace memorial,
        past the big brass doors of Brooklyn's Main
Library before heading downhill to Atlantic
        Avenue's Long Island station; I'd imagine
an Elvis tune to try on my trumpet someday
        for Jimmy Morris, "*I want you, I need you,*
I love you," though, thus far I only managed
        "*We Three Kings of Orient.*" I fell in love
with Jimmy when 4th graders, when the boys'
        class paraded into Holy Cross auditorium,

13

while we girls waited listening to Miss Weber
      play the piano for our ballroom dance class
to begin, though I never danced with Jimmy since
      he was tall and I was small; partners assigned
according to height, so freckled-face Allen and I
      danced awkwardly on Tuesdays for five years.
While Jimmy partnered with beautiful Margaret
      McAlae; they went on to the best Catholic
high schools, he to the Jesuits' Brooklyn Prep,
      she to Bishop McDonnell's, Natalie and I
to middle class St. Joseph's High which was
      surprisingly booked with Jimmy's school
for our graduation trip on the Hudson River
      Circle Line to Bear Mountain. Rock and Roll
belted across the ship's shiny dance floor-- *Elvis,*
      Little Richard, The Platters, The Supremes, Fats
Domino, the Everly Brothers. Engines humming
      below deck. We girls danced *the Lindy* and *Slide,*
while the boys watched as they leaned against
      the wall. Natalie and I climbed the silvery stairs
to the upper deck as the boat sailed back to the city,
      gliding past the Palisades' golden cliffs, under
the George Washington Bridge's lights as if it were
      a necklace glowing in the gathering dark. Trumpet
notes drifted on warm April air currents, reviving
      my musical ambitions, when I first joined the high
school orchestra, pressing the three silvery valves,
      tightening and loosening my lips. Practicing at
home was almost impossible, as my brothers shouted:
      "Shut up!" which I did and didn't do before doing
it again. Using *the mute* muffled my notes, so they
      sounded as if I played underwater. Powerful
bellowing, shyly softening, shaping a tempo inside
      my daydreams of dancing with Jimmy. I owed
my trumpet skills, such as they were, to Mr. Renner,
      who conducted our school orchestra so seriously

you'd think we were a miniature philharmonic--
"*Altogether now!*" as his hair fell over his face.
Suddenly he'd stop to correct a girl, calling across
the winds and violins: "*Miss Cook play those high
notes again at the beginning of the measure. Everyone
now!*" Pressing the valves and blowing softly,
if at all, surprised by his: "*Much better!* " I went
on to play trumpet in the convent band, eight
sisters entertaining at Christmas, Saint Patrick's
Day and Easter. Practice was a welcome way
to avoid washing dishes, studying, or weeding
the cemetery. After the convent, my husband's
birthday gift was a silver trumpet, played by his
friend Chuck Cameron in Broadway's "*Hello
Dolly*." I've managed a few muffled notes for
grandkids-- laughter, shouting "*More! More!*"

SURVIVAL SKILLS, RIIS PARK BEACH

At age five or six I nearly drowned in Lake
Ronkonkoma, Long Island, having ignored
my father's warning--- "*Carolyn! Don't go
any further!*" Daring to disobey, I suddenly
slipped into deep cloudy waters, waking later
in sunlight on the blanket beside my mother.
"*Dad saved you just in time!*" The following
week he drove us down Flatbush Avenue,
through the Flatlands, past Star of the Sea
parish, Floyd Benet Air Field, then across
the Jamaica Bay drawbridge into a huge
parking lot. My brothers Richie and John
jumped out of the car, while I held grandma's
hand as she exclaimed-- "*Ah, breathe in
the sea air, as when I was a girl in Aberdeen!*"
We carried towels, paper bags, a thermos
and blankets while Dad tucked the big umbrella

15

under his arm. Grandpa, as usual, was dressed
in a suit as he shuffled along. I tiptoed barefoot
    to avoid the boardwalk splinters, then jumped
spot-to-spot on the hot white sand. Dad looked
    carefully for a private place amid the crowd,
where he pitched the umbrella atop the slope,
    yet near enough to see the surf. Ah, those
wild rolling waves, rippling lines my brothers
    and I ran close to, then away, playing "*Water
can't catch me.*" Grandma splashed her shoulders
    as she held tightly to the thick rope dividing
our beach. One at a time, Dad taught Richie,
    John and me the dog paddle*: "Cup your hands,
take small underwater strokes. Keep your head high
    and you'll do fine.*" He held me by the straps
of my bathing suit, before slowly letting go, so
    I bobbed duck-like over the waves. Soon
Richie was diving into *the big ones.* John and I
    followed tentatively. Ah, the hissing bubbling
rumble within a wave, its crashing roar coming
    into calm. Jumping, diving, gliding. Lunch
on the blanket, I'd watch Dad's graceful arching
    arms as he swam past the jetty, vanishing till
he appeared on the next beach, riding waves to shore.
    Lifeguards always ran towards any call for:
"*Help!*" And we kids pushed into the crowd circling
    a lifeguard's intense attempts at saving someone,
mouth-to-mouth resuscitation, lifting their arms,
    pressing their chest, then rushing the victim
on a stretcher to an ambulance on the boardwalk.
    If lightning flashed in dark clouds brewing over
the horizon, everyone was waved from the surf.
    We'd toss our things into the blanket, then rush
to the car. Such haste was frightening for a child,
    though it was later in life I learned my parents
stood close to people who were killed by lightning

16

at this beach. Heading home across Jamaica Bay's
sparkling waters visible through the steel rods of
    the drawbridge; if a big boat neared, I'd plead:
"Hurry Dad! The bridge will open!" Richie and John
    laughed. Often we'd stop at the Nostrand Avenue's
Jewish Deli. We kids took turns using the silvery tongs
    to fish for kosher pickles in a wooden barrel. Soon
home, I'd flop on my bed, tingling sand stuck between
    my toes, then I'd gaze through our open apartment
window seeing seagulls winging their way over Flatbush
    Avenue heading towards the nearby Atlantic.

At fourteen I stopped going with my family to
    Riis Park beach, since I was away all summer
as a counselor-aide at Camp Oh-Neh-Tah, earning
    a Red Cross lifeguard card: practicing rescues
of girls who pretended to be drowning, so I'd swim
    fast, turn the girl round, rest her on my hip, and
do the sidestroke to shore. I never rescued anyone
    in *real life*, unless saving myself from harm in
grade school, when a nun made us stand before class
    and say whether we were Irish or not. Didn't our
family name *Cook* sound *English;* the worse fate I
    feared as a child in this Irish Catholic school.
I learned Dad's grandpa changed his family name
    Koch to *Cook* after leaving Germany, before
enlisting in the Union Army. (Wasn't Mayor Koch
    Jewish; why not us?) I hid the *biggest* secret--
that Uncle Howard uncovered in New York City's
    public records: we were descendants of *Mary
Ball Washington,* so nuns at school might suspect
    my mother and grand-parents were *converts,*
meaning once-upon-a-time *Protestants* (which
    they were!) God forbid such a revelation about
my relatives, since our school rules frowned on
    contact with Protestants, forbidding us to join

17

the Girl Scouts, since their meetings were held in
        the basement of the Dutch Reformed church
on Flatbush Avenue. I always acted as if I was *Irish*;
        besides my other grandma, *Nana*, Margaret
Drury was *Irish,* only she wasn't a blood relative,
        rather a family friend, who raised Dad, Aunt
Muriel and Uncle John, after their mother died.
        I always wore green and marched with Natalie
(my Polish classmate) in the Saint Patrick's Day
        parade along Fifth Avenue, simply slipping into
a clan singing familiar Irish songs. At camp no one
        asked us to reveal our ethnicity. Surprising
(in hindsight) my entering the convent, since most
        members were *Irish and proud of it!* Perhaps
my (unconscious) wish *to belong*? Remembering
        our Hanley neighbors' parties for their eleven
kids' Baptisms, First Communions, Confirmations.
        Mr. Hanley began with *"Danny Boy."* Judy,
Barbara, and I did an Irish jig. My Mom, Dad,
        and everyone else enjoyed the Hanley's Irish
hospitality. Looking back, decades later, I see
        how welcomed I always was, as if a member
of this family. So tis true in my heart and soul:
        I am, indeed, Irish, ever after as to this day,
in touch with Judy and Barbara, like close cousins.

II

CONVENT

"Let your own voice, assured and bold and free,
Ring out, give wish a tongue, give will a word;
Then will I speak what I'm ordained to say."
Dante, *Paradiso, Canto XV*

"We for Love's clergy are only instruments;
.   .   .   In this our universe,
.   .   .   Since all divine
Is love or wonder   .   .   ."
John Donne, *Elegy XX*

THE NOVITIATE, TOPSFIELD, MASSACHUSETTS

1.

Waving goodbye to our families, we were
    leaving the motherhouse by bus heading
to a new novitiate in the forests of Topsfield,
    Massachusetts, for our *Canonical Year,*
supposedly *the most difficult* one on the path
    to becoming a Maryknoll missioner. No
radios, TV, newspapers or phones allowed.
    Family visits only twice a year. Letters
limited to one a week, none during Lent
    and Advent. We heard tales told by
senior novices about Sister Paul Miriam,
    the Novice mistress's strict ways. Were
they exaggerating about her reputation?
    She loomed in my mind as a Marine
sergeant might for recruits, a task master,
    who'd weed the wheat from the chaff--
"Sister, you'll need to leave. This vocation isn't
    for you." Young and impressionable,
as I was, wanting to be wanted and dreading
    she might say *"Pack your bags!"* On a visiting
Sunday in August, Mom and Dad arrived with
    my brother Richie and his wife Loretta,
who recently returned from their honeymoon
    in Puerto Rico; first of our family to travel
by plane. Newlyweds laughing and holding
    hands. I felt awkward in a grey woolen tunic
and white starched veil framing my face. Soon
    the novitiate bell boomed across the lawn.
Time to say goodbye. I waved as Richie drove
    his maroon Buick, past the roses I weeded
yesterday, slowly disappearing past the gate.

2.

Wednesdays we hiked into the woods with
    Sister Paul Miriam. Frequently she'd jump
for joy on hearing a warbler, thrush, scarlet
    tanager or chickadee. She knew each bird by
their song, coloring and flight. Strolling the cloister
    halls, she'd swing her arms in a happy-go-lucky
way. After reporting my weekly infractions of
    breaking *The Rule*, she'd look at me nonchalantly,
as if implying *not a big deal,* while she'd turn toward
    the window-- "*See, the sparrows love the branch*
I placed next to their feeder." Yes, a passionate
    nature lover, also fine painter and she possessed
an adventurous spirit. Instead of being assigned
    to Latin America, Africa or Asia, her superiors
kept her as novice mistress for more than twenty
    years. Were her ironic comments, quick wit
and almost casual attitude at times about rules
    a cloak concealing her frustration at being cooped
up in a routine of correcting novices and the difficult
    task of deciding who didn't belong, who to send
home. Once in early Spring, she knelt on the damp
    earth under an ancient pine, shouting-- "*Look!*
The crocuses are back!" as she stroked their fresh
    yellow, pink, white and purple petals; her face
glowing with an ecstasy sometimes seen in chapel.

SISTER ITA FORD M.M.

On December 2, 1980 Sisters Ita Ford, Maura Clark,
    Dorothy Kazel and Jean Donovan were raped,
murdered and tossed into a shallow grave by
    members of a Salvadoran death squad. I knew
Ita in Maryknoll. She was witty, smart, mischievous.

21

We both hailed from Brooklyn. (In 1952 Ita's great-
uncle Bishop Francis Ford died in a Chinese prison.)
Ita served the poor in Chile along with her close
friend Sister Carla Piette, till they answered the call
of Archbishop Oscar Romero's for Spanish-
speaking missioners to provide sanctuaries for war
refugees in El Salvador. Carla arrived March 24,
1980 (the day Romero was assassinated while he was
offering Mass). Ita joined Carla in Chalatenango,
where they delivered food to families forced into
hiding, shuttled women and children between
safe houses as the military violence intensified.
One day they were driving a recently released
prisoner to his village. Suddenly a flash-flood
the car. Carla pushed Ita out the window to safety,
though she herself drowned. Overcome by grief,
Ita retreated to the motherhouse, wondering
why she was spared. Then realizing the risk, she
requested reassignment to El Salvador. Not
long afterwards, Ita, Dorothy, Maura and Jean
were ambushed, raped, murdered, and tossed
into shallow graves. Over twenty years later,
Sister Lil Mattingly crossed "*the line*" at Fort
Benning, Georgia, as an act of civil disobedience
to protest the US government's training of
Latin American military, who led death-squads
that tortured and murdered innocents, as Ita,
her sisters, Oscar Romero and countless others.
Lil served six months in a Danbury, Connecticut
prison. She is a soft-spoken Kentuckian nurse
with a broad smile and gentle manner that
gives no hint of her strong determination to
speak truth to those in power, including
American authorities, who violate human rights.

IPSWITCH BIRD SANCTUARY MASSACHUSETTS

Clouds were drifting across a wide blue sky over
    the wild wheat fields of the Bird Sanctuary. Sap
dripped down pine trees. Willows were waving
    by the stream during those years, when I was
in my early twenties, preparing for Profession Day
    during our Novitiate training. Allowed an afternoon
off each week for hiking, reading, daydreaming, relaxing.
    A group of us often went to the ledge overlooking
the Rockery's silvery pond. We shared dreams for
    future missions to Africa, Central or South America,
the Pacific Islands, Philippines to serve the poor as
    a social worker, teacher, community organizer,
catechist, nurse, or doctor. Linda longed to visit her
    family in Saugerties. No one mentioned missing
the world, code for *life outside the convent.* Mary Jane
    spoke nostalgically of her college years. Everyone
laughed at Beth's stories of working at Seagram's
    in New York City. Helen sketched *the ruins,*
an abandoned estate we hiked through on our way
    to the Bird Sanctuary. She drew a couple on
the terrace overlooking the apple orchard. Did
    she have a romantic past? Did any of us? We
chased each other through the fields, tumbling
    onto a soft blanket of wheat, the way kids fall
with their arms open wide as angels in the snow.
    Red-tailed hawks flew by, bees buzzed round
our fingers, finches darting across our faces, earth's
    warmth beneath us. Our spell broken by
Connie calling: *"Hurry! We'll be late for chapel!"*
    Rushing to the gate, I turned for a last look
before running after my sisters, veil flying,
    dogs chasing, rosary catching on brambles.
Breathless in chapel, Linda smiled across the aisle,
    as we began the psalms, bowing to each other.

23

BRIDES OF CHRIST

On Good Friday a makeshift white tent was set
    up for a temporary tabernacle outside our chapel
signifying Christ's entombment. Easter lilies hid
    in alcoves, their sweet pungent scent wafting
through the corridors of our convent. In the silence
    I wondered how Christ could espouse Himself
to each of us on Profession Day? Doubts swirled.
    Was our bond as Christ's bride simply a metaphor?
Why weren't our vows equally valuable as a sacrament
    in the way ordination was for men? Such an idyllic,
almost *romantic* setting for day-dreaming by the Topsfield,
    Massachusetts forest; similarly, the country setting
for our motherhouse outside Ossining, New York.
    Across the road such an awesome green-tiled
seminary roof, red eaves curving up in a Far Eastern
    flare atop Sunset Hill, highest site in Westchester
county overlooking the Hudson opposite the amber
    cliffs of the Palisades. Apple orchards, wheat fields,
perfect setting for daydreaming during retreats. No
    friendships permitted between the sexes. Sparrows
were foraging in raspberry bushes outside my cell
    window one snowy Sunday. Pine branches
sparkling. A fox trotting along the rocks framing
    Our Lady's shrine. A subtle *divine presence* I first
felt as a child at summer camp in the Catskills, city
    girls holding hands under the dark filled stars.

CLARE AND FRANCIS OF ASSISI

Saying goodbye to him is almost too much to bear.
Am I sounding overly dramatic? Dear God, do you

Understand how close we were? Of course, since
You were the one who brought us together. Am I

Ungrateful? I didn't realize at the beginning he'd
Remain working in the world, while I'd be called to

Enter the cloister. Do I doubt the value of prayer?
Am I sounding skeptical? *Why me? Why not*

Someone else behind the grille? I'd rather lead
An *active life* serving others alongside him. He

Asked me to take Perpetual vows in an enclosure.
Sealed into this Sanctuary for life. Why my gloomy

Attitude?   Sacrifice is easier said than done. My life
Will be a hidden one and far from Francis. You ask

Where's my faith in Your presence? You wonder
Why You aren't enough? Help me believe my prayers

Make a difference in the lives of others, in his life.
Ravish me with Your divine love so I can let him go.

CLARE'S PRAYER

Keep me in the palm of your hand. Protect me
From envy and the wish to have what is not meant

To be mine. Help me stay faithful to Your plan.
Day and night I pray to discern Your design.

Your absence is not easy. My heart hurts, yet I struggle
To accept things as they are. I pray for his success

Serving the poor, healing lepers, preaching in towns far
From home. I live in joyful expectation of sharing

Bread and wine in community with him at the crossroads,
Where the sick come for comfort, elders are protected,

Widows consoled, children celebrated. He has gone
Down the road, where the town ends and the fields go

Golden as far as the eye can see. Our last time together
I felt on fire. Hot coals in my soul. Sun singing in

My heart. I stayed silent. Others surrounding us.
I pretended my life within the cloister was easy.

Whatever will be will be. Looking forward to seeing
Him lifts my spirit in prayer and gratitude. Alleluia.

PASSOVER

At midnight the moon disappears in clouds
     over the olive grove. Drops of blood fall
from his forehead. Loud voices are coming
     closer. Is he going to lose everything they
worked for? A cock crows three times. Peter
     draws his sword. Judas kisses his face.
Lavender and rosemary stick to our clothes
     as we run away, spend the night hiding,
praying for courage, though we do nothing to
     save him. Soldiers shout: *"Criminal! Traitor!"*
They torture and throw him into prison. He is
     left to face death alone, while we, his friends,
abandon him in the hour of his greatest need.

MAGDALENE

He's vanished. Where is he? Will we meet again,
  or is it too late?   Who is this man who avoids
  answering-- *"Where are they hiding him?"*
*"Let me touch you, kiss your hands, warm your feet.
  Let me hug you close and closer." "No. Not now.
  Later. Later. There are others I need to see."*
Does he think in telling me this I'll understand
  and not be upset? I pretend I'm fine. After all,
  what can I do? He will do what he needs to do,
no matter what I say. Best to stay silent. *"Yes.
  Sure. See you later."* When will *"later"* be?
  In the afterwards of waiting-- how quiet
the olive grove. Is he with John and James?
  Are they cooking fish over an outdoor fire,
  drinking wine together? Is Thomas pressing
his side? Is John leaning on his heart? I'm
  supposed to stay inside with the women,
  waiting for his return. When will he come?

You have come back to us . . .
  I touch your side and hands, feel
  the marks of your agony, recalling
that morning we walked round the lake
  under the cypresses on the opposite shore,
  as olive groves stood in a semi-circle,
gray discs gleamed along Lake Galilee.
  Do we remember words sealed with a kiss,
  while the sun rose over the garden wall. You
had returned a changed man. Suffering visible
  in your face, hands roughened, scars on your
  body as if you were caught in an electric
storm. You went through hell and came back.
  Some say you suffered and died, all was over,
  finished, failed. How wrong the naysayers.

I see your eyes in the stars, feel your heart
    beating in earth's pulse, hear you calling
the names of ancestors across the mountain.

"DO THIS IN MEMORY OF ME"
in memory of Joseph

Since you've gone, some advise *letting go*,
    as if accepting loss bestows forgetfulness,
or laughter becomes *the best medicine* for
    banishing grief. I prefer reenacting Christ's
comforting words: *"Do this in memory of me."*
    Recalling our 44 years *together*-- caring
for our sons, vacation adventures, wintry
    mulch of sicknesses, hibernating cave of
our love's intimacy, pink white snowflake
    flowers falling from almond and plum
orchards as we arrived in the Valley of Heart's
    delight, welcoming poppies lining the green
hills of Stanford along 280 to and from San
    Francisco, mix of family, friends, community,
works in the world, weaving us close closer,
    water fountain singing near our San Jose
Rose garden, daffodil bouquets during Lent
    at the grocery store, Good Friday's loss
eased three days later by Easter lilies filling
    alcoves of the Mission chapel, palm trees
dancing *Alleluias* along San Jose's *Alameda.*

THÉRÈSE OF LISIEUX, PROFESSION DAY

If I give myself to God in final vows
    will my sacrifice matter to anyone
other than the One who receives my
    devotion? I was not forced into
religious life. After vows, will I feel

changed physically, mentally,
spiritually? Further down the road,
    will I regret giving up the world?
Can I be sure this community life
    will sustain me twenty years later?
If I express doubts to my superiors,
    will they ask me to leave? I'll throw
caution to the wind. Embrace this *calling*
    that I first felt at age fifteen. Alleluia.

HEART AND SOUL, SANTA CLARA UNIVERSITY
in memory of Theodore Mackin S.J.

After Ordination, you studied Theology for three years
    at the Gregorian in Rome. Sunday afternoon strolls.
    Geraniums overflow terra-cotta bowls. Grape vines

woven in Bacchus' beard. Pan playing his flute. Stone
    stairs leading into the Borghese gardens. Apollo
    chasing Daphne in a laurel grove. Neptune laughing

with nymphs teasing him in the Trevi fountain. Were
    there temptations, at times, with a life other than
    the one you were called to at age eighteen. Years later

your vocation's complicated. You've known Teresa's
    ecstasy and John of the Cross's dark night of the soul.
    Your white and red Pentecostal robes, your purple

Lenten and Advent stole. You kiss the altar stone,
    lead liturgies, teach courses on marriage. You're
    a canon lawyer pleading with the church to annul

hopeless relationships. Will you seek absolution if you
leave the Order? Your young hands raised the sacred
bread and wine. Over thirty years teaching at Santa

Clara University, where wisteria, cyclamens, crocuses,
and roses fill the gardens. Hummingbirds sip nectar
from fuchsias. The Mission bell rings for daily Mass

and Saturday weddings. Students seek your counsel,
yet who can you confide in . . . *Why after all these*
years? Will I leave my brothers, my family, my friends?

Love is making a personal appeal. Indecision's a thorn
in your side. You console the grieving, comfort the
sick, celebrate marriages of friends and relatives.

Hope is a candle you light in the darkened vestibule at
each Easter Vigil, plunge the honeyed beeswax into
Baptismal waters, marking its cream-colored body

with red and green letters hailing Christ Alpha and
Omega. You rub oil on a baby's forehead, perhaps
wish the child was yours. Bougainvillea by the path

bordering Nobili residence, where you live with fellow
Jesuits. Olive trees surround the adobe patio,
where meals are taken on summer days. You prune

the Mission roses with your fingers on the way to class.
If you leave you'll go quietly. No goodbyes. No
apologies. No explanations. Yet, you'll never forget

these brothers and sisters, this chapel and rituals, these
families, friends, colleagues, students, roses, this
community, this Santa Clara University campus.

Explaining your dilemma is difficult. You leave San Jose
　　when the wisteria's at its height along the adobe walls.
　　A few months later a postcard arrives: you've found

new happiness. Having given up everything, you are
　　honeymooning in Italy. Apollo still pursues Daphne
　　in the Villa Borghese gardens within sight of Saint

Peter's brooding dome. The Bay of Naples's smoking
　　Vesuvius seen from ship when you arrived as
　　a young priest; desire and devotion were smoldering

in your heart and soul. You died of prostate cancer
　　three years after your marriage. Mass at Georgetown
　　where you used to sing in the choir and your memory

celebrated at a Eucharist at Mission Santa Clara University.
　　Your wife offered the homily. Church packed with
　　students, faculty, friends, family and local community.

III

TERESA DE AVILA,
JUAN DE LA CRUZ

"Could I in-thee as thou in- me thee . . .
Whence she to whom my whole self open was
As to myself . . ."
Dante, *Paradiso, Cantos I & IX*

"You must fly with the plumes . . . And be lifted up
On the wings of desire . . ."
Dante, *Purgatorio, Canto IV*

". . . it is in the nature of love to discern the good,
and the best love is, in some part, a love of what is
good. Ducane was very conscious, that he and Mary
communicated by means of what was good in them."
Iris Murdoch, *The Nice and the Good*

AVILA

Avila, city of my birth, your fortress-like walls
    rise across the plains. Your towers pierce
the sky. Sun streaks down your dark side streets.
    Olives, rosemary, lavender and thyme ripen
in your cloister gardens. Moonlight skips over
    the cobblestones of your remote courtyards.
Sanctuary lamp burning before me at midnight's
    Holy Hour. This tonic of triple vows is a stringent
antidote for wayward spirits as mine. Regulations
    reign supreme. Spontaneities suppressed.
Voluntary vows-- Poverty, Chastity, Obedience;
    why complain? Challenges abound, a guide for
others, even if I lose my direction. Our vocation calls
    for every ounce of discernment. My mercurial
nature rebels. I should practice what I preach.
    *"Change what needs changing. Embrace what
can't be changed. Discern the difference . . ."*

SECRETS

Rumors spread about his strange, wild
    ways. Some call him a *madman*. He
is supposedly passionate about prayer,
    bravely criticizes church authority.
Why would I feel compelled to meet such
    a man? Are we similar? My motives
are mysterious, even to myself. What
    do I hope will happen? How decide
if God desires our meeting? At night
    the obstacles seem insurmountable.
Expectations exceed my gifts to serve
    family, friends, and the community.
After Compline, I'll close my cell door,
    light a candle and write him secretly.

JUAN DE LA CRUZ

Fortunately, my confessor asks me
      to carry letters and several books
for the Carmelite monastery, since
      he knows I'll be passing by Toledo
on my way to visiting our sisters at
      various convents. I'll eagerly hike
the miles while praying the syllables
      of his name . . . *Juan de la Cruz.*

THE RULE

Some sisters say I'm too easy going--
      "Mother, many feel you fail to insist
that sisters follow the Rule strictly. You
      should speak to the community, demand
obedience, give harsh penances, so you'll be
      taken seriously." Quite the opposite of
those who complain I'm too strict. Is a
      middle path possible, a golden mean
desirable, or will I compromise myself
      in pleasing these factions? *"Conformity*
is not our goal. Fear is not freedom. Christ's
      example-- renounce the temptations of
power over others, or prestige at the expense of
      another, offer hospitality to strangers, tend
the sick, welcome the poor, comfort widows,
      play with children, learn from your mistakes."

BENEDICTION

Señor of the purple grapes and glistening
      apricots, your sun pierces thick fog.
Shafts of golden light burn inside your

roses. Honeysuckle perfumes our
garden. Dark red wine refreshes for
     feast days. Tomatoes, olives, onions,
garlic, almonds, warm bread grace our
     table. Thunder shatters *Profound Silence*.
Lightning penetrates this dark enclosure.
     Sweet rain relieving the parched earth.
Jasmine stars swimming within green tea
     in our cups. Doves cooing under eaves.
Honeybees tumbling in lavender. We're
     singing psalms across the aisle, as if
a single voice at Vespers. I pray you'll
     reappear in a blissful dream tonight.

OCCUPYING A CELL

Rumors circulate throughout the country
     about his defiant ways. Some claim he
spends hours in a cave praying without his
     superiors' permission. They will throw
him into prison, prevent others from following
     his example. Authorities fear losing power.
They need complacent lambs obeying their
     orders. His independent ways undermine
their wish to control. *"Who does he think
     he is! Pride's a sin. Let's confiscate his
writing materials. Burn all his poetry."*

ON THE WAY

How hot the stones under my feet. Only
     a few more miles. What will I say? Will
he understand? I place my trust in the One
     who calls us to serve His cause. I'll rest
in the olive grove alongside the monastery

before knocking on the door. "*Pase
adelante mi hermana*." Sparks flickering
        in his dark eyes, his glance, his words
strike as arrows into my soul. Am I falling
        in love with him? God forbid such a fate!
I don't know if he thinks of me in the way
        I'm thinking of him. I shouldn't care,
but I do. My heart's racing when we're
        together, same pleasurable feeling
I sometimes experience during prayer.

MORNING MEDITATION

His poetry flows through me in waves of
        amazement during morning meditation.
Knowing we share the sacred bread and wine,
        although we're miles apart, stirs my faith,
arouses my hope. Daily distractions pull me
        back to ordinary responsibilities. Some
complain about annoying incidentals. Others
        are caught in a crisis of faith. I'm impatient
trying to discipline my wandering mind, when
        memories of our times together make me
smile. Letting go, yet hoping for a reunion,
        trusting God's love casts a spell whether
we wished for that or not. Yes, surrender . . .

MI CORAZÓN

My heart's full of expectation. My soul's spinning
        in confusion. My mind counsels calm as I pace

the courtyard. Deciphering God's desire is difficult.
        I'm scorched by imagining this man's affection.

Daily challenges of community life continue. Am I
  seeking something forbidden? Has he made

room in his heart for me? Embarrassing to express
  these emotions, after all, I'm trained to *let go*, not

expect anything. *Practice detachment* is what I preach,
  yet longing flies as a bird through the windows

of my eyes when Juan appears on the road. Forget-me-
  nots proliferate in my memory, recalling his familiar

footsteps in our garden. I'm sipping chestnut tea to chase
  away worry, star of Bethlehem essence to heal loss,

pressed olives to restore my strength. An angel smiles
  on the sanctuary wall pointing to the open door.

MIDNIGHT MEDITATION

Recalling his footsteps on the path outside my window

on his way to offer Mass at our convent. During midnight

meditation, I seek his presence in prayer. Far more difficult

than I imagined to bring him back after he has gone . . .

Remembering the things he loved: foxes, quails, roses,

humming birds, olives, oaks, laurels, caves, mountain tops.

He is nowhere in sight. This is the dark night of my soul.

I've pressed wildflowers inside my missal, those we

37

picked in the fields outside the city walls one day when

he lifted a stray lamb to his heart, saying: *"Be not afraid."*

DAYDREAMING

A summer afternoon beyond the city
    walls. You are dressed in black.
Dark clouds cover the mountains.

Thunder rumbles along high ridges.
    Bolts of lightning shoot across
the valley. You love these wild

storms. Freedom to find unknown
    trails. A cave no one else has
discovered. Shared memories smolder

in my soul. Are these scars on your
    hands from when they threw you
into prison? Not one to complain, you

smile when I ask for details. At night
    savoring your words simmering
within the lines of your writing, flying

like birds settling in the nest of my heart.
    Lenten ashes of sacrifice burst into
the flamed- tongue Dove lighting every

corner of my being. Discipline is supposedly
    crucial to our religious roles. What
if my community knew how I felt after

Mass, when setting plates of sweet figs,
     cheese, olives, tomatoes, warm bread
and wine for your meal, then watching

through the window while you walk
     in the mustard field, tiny yellow buds
blooming by your finger-tips, bees round

the lavender, almonds shedding furry green
     enclosures, olives proudly in shiny black
skins. Your compassionate sweet smile.

SOLITARY CONFINEMENT

Though we're separated by prison walls,
no one can prevent us from staying in touch
     through prayer. Faith keeps hope alive in
Love. I dream us together in the olive grove.
     Moonlight pierces the clouds and enters
my cell. I pretend an angel's carrying my letter
     tucked in an arrow quiver aimed at his heart.
Though tortured in prison they can't break his
     spirit. Yes, I'll continue imagining us chanting
Compline together in choir. Doves in the eaves.
     He hides paper, pen and an ink vial beneath
a straw mattress. I pray for his smuggled note:
     "Querida, I'll meet you at the mountain top."

AFTER RELEASE

At morning meditation, I hear his footsteps
     on the stone path leading into our chapel.
Soon thunder claps shake the walls. Lightning
     fills our dark cloister corridors. He changes
old clothes for a white chasuble. Handsome
     in candle light as he bends over the altar and

raises his arms elevating the sacred bread and
      wine. He looks thin and exhausted. In line
for communion, I look at him closer, our first
      meeting since his release from prison. A personal
greeting is impossible. He leaves immediately
      after Mass. During breakfast I hear the gate bang.
I pretend calm, while worrying if he was harmed?
      Why imprisoned and for so long? Envy of his gifts
poisoned the hearts of the persecutors. I take comfort
      in doves bathing in the fountain, lavender scenting
the garden, olives and almonds ripening and best
      of all-- an envelope slipped under my door. I tear it
open: "*Querida Teresita.*" He plans a hike to his
      cave tomorrow and wishes to pray with me there.

"HASTA LUEGO"

A summer afternoon. You're wearing a black cloak.
      Clouds conceal the cathedral towers. Thunder
rumbles through the valley. Hot stones steaming.

You're released from jail. Scars visible on your hands.
      Our visit is limited. We're being watched. Formality
cloaks our conversation. Not the way it was when

we leapt across a raging river, laughing as though
      we're children. At night I delight in your words
as they dance on the pages. Am I jealous of God's

hold on you? We will follow His call. If I lose you,
      the foundations of my faith will not shatter. I try to
trust providential care and rely upon the kindness of

the Holy Spirit to carry our communion. At prayer
      you're near, yet far. Water mingles with wine,
bread's changed into divine matter. I long to rub

sacred oil on your scars. Steadfast in our vocations.
Will we picnic again? Sweet figs, olives, tomatoes
and red wine. We petted the goat's gleaming fur.

Hawks were fleeing a storm. Believing, in the end,
nothing can keep us apart, though the path through
the valley is treacherous, we will come through . . .

SISTERS AND BROTHERS

We will not close ourselves off, instead stay open
to our sisters and brothers, sharing their grief,

celebrating their joys, revealing our own weakness
and vulnerability. Prayer and service will nourish

our body and soul. Take time to visit prisoners,
play with children, celebrate feast days, offer

a refuge for the homeless, nurture mother earth,
protect animals, comfort widows, practice

gratefulness, trusting in the kindness of strangers,
peace a priority, nurturing mercy, social-justice,

reconciliation. Undeterred by defeat. Learning
joy from the little ones. Keeping embers of hope

alive on the darkest days. Believing death is not
an end. Our love leaps across the great divide.

VAYA CON DÍOS

Olive groves, grape vineyards, dusty country roads.
      An abandoned chapel. Sunlight streamed across
the shattered floor. A distant village's guitar music,
      castanets, wedding songs. Our letters carried
secretly by friends, since our superiors practice
      surveillance prescribed by: "*The Rule.*" Joyful
surprise when I praise your poem. Encouraging
      the arts is forbidden. The sin of pride must be
prevented. Silence is a stinging rebuke. "*How dare
      he waste time writing! Who does he think he is,
someone special? We'll teach him a lesson he won't
      forget. We'll isolate him in prison.*" They are
ignorant of the hours you struggle with words,
      lines, stanzas, facing fear, leaping across abysses,
exploring dark forests. Desire wrestles with doubt,
      since you seek the Divine in love's unpredictable
adventure. Mountain vistas, owl calls at midnight,
      ministries to the poor, sick, elderly and children.
Shared memories shape a sanctuary in our souls. Rain
      splashing through the ceiling of an abandoned
chapel. I jumped at thunder blasts! Your beard was
      glistening in lightning flashes. Graceful arc
of your shoulders bending to kiss the rustic figure
      of Christ the Good Shepherd. "*Vaya con Dios,
Juan.*" "*Vaya con Dios, mi Teresita. Hasta luego . . .*"

IV

CALIFORNIA

"Now in the hour that melts with homesick yearning
   The hearts of seafarers who've had to say
   Farewell to those they love, that very morning--"
      Dante, *Purgatorio, Canto III*

"I remember when the brown evening was dripping into
the mountain hollow, and I suddenly felt, as I watched it
turning under its own sky into the shady night with all its
animals asleep in their caves, that I too was a living part
of it, of a home without walls or boundary where anyone
might wander, a single pattern with no great division"
      Freya Stark, *The Minaret of Djam,*
      An Excursion in Afghanistan

FIELD TRIP, GOLDEN GATE PARK
for Eddie and Peter

Santa Clara's Westwood Open's 4th grade field
    trip with Eddie and Peter's classmates, teachers
Steve and Bob, plus several parents as myself, to
    the Fragrance Garden in Golden Gate Park's
Arboretum. The kids were encouraged to: *"Touch*
    and smell the lavender, rosemary, fennel, salvia,
chamomile and lamb's ear plants." Greg and Max
    rang a large rusty bell, relic of California's early
days, subject of their social studies project. Suddenly
    Peter began hopping along a ledge surrounding
the fountain. Falling in, dripping wet, he ran into
    the Australian Rainforest, emerging to everyone's
applause: *"Peter's wearing Kristin's shorts!"* Unfazed,
    he did dazzling break dance spins, prefiguring his
future in Theatre Arts at Fordham University's Lincoln
    Center. I tucked sprigs of lavender and ivy geranium
in my pocket, now flourishing in our San Jose garden.

OFF TO COLLEGE, FORDHAM UNIVERSITY, NYC

In a few days Peter starts as a freshman at Fordham's
Lincoln Center campus. We're crossing West 78th &

Amsterdam Avenue. *"Hey, Mom, why rush?"* *"I'm from*
New York! This isn't San Francisco! Cars jump the lights."

We reach Hotel Lucern, where Fordham's rented three
floors to house Theatre Arts students. A tiny elevator takes

us to the 6th floor. Peter's roommate Bobby's listens to
Les Miserables. *"I hope to make it on Broadway."* His Mom

phoned me in May. *"Bobby's our youngest. We're hoping his asthma doesn't act up in New York, so far from Maryland."*

I thought her overly protective. By Christmas break,
I'd feel similarly after overhearing Peter telling friends

how his hair froze when walking sixteen city streets to
classes. Later on. I asked: *"Don't you take the school shuttle?"*

"I get up too late." (Mary Jeanne clues me in: *"Typical
Theatre Arts major! Late nights, late mornings"*) Home for

the summer, Peter casually says: *"After working at
Bloomingdale's, I walk from Lexington Avenue and East 52nd*

past the Plaza Hotel." *"But there's a cross-town bus through
Central Park!"* *"It's okay. I didn't know there was one."*

His tales to cousins at a family dinner: *"Once a guy followed
me after night class, his sandals swishing on the sidewalk, so*

*I ducked into a grocery store and the owner's brother walked me
back to the hotel. Once when I was with friends on the subway*

*in Brooklyn at two in the morning, some guys started staring
us down. So, we tried not to look worried."* I try not to look

worried driving Peter to SFO. Putting on a reassuring
smile, I wave goodbye: *"Enjoy school, and give my regards*

to Broadway!" For his junior year, he chooses Santa Clara
University. *"I miss the warm weather; I'll be back to Fordham*

as a senior." Unwrapped blue sheets fall from his suitcase.
"Didn't we buy these two years ago?" *"Yeah, I never used*

45

*them, since the laundry across the street costs almost the same as
doing it in the hotel basement. Besides the laundry folds it all."*

Peter stays on at SCU, perhaps in love with a coed?
Dad Joe says: *"Never underestimate California's climate!"*

HOMELESS IN PALO ALTO, CALIFORNIA

I'm waiting in a Palo Alto cafe for my son
    Peter, who'll arrive soon for lunch.
A casual place-- you order at the counter,
    take a number and wait for your drink,
soup, salad, or sandwich. I'm sitting near
    the window. My table's an inch away
from a young man who sleeps sideways
    on his folded arms at the outdoor table.
I'm near enough to see his delicate eyebrows,
    finely formed small ears and his long
tapered fingers. By his feet a dirty backpack
    and crumpled quilt. What were his
mother's feelings the day he was born?
    His dark silky hair, curly eye lashes,
beautiful mouth. Did he walk at an early
    age? Was he a talkative or quiet child?
Did he attend nearby Stanford or Foothill
    Community College? Or was college
never an option for him? Is he Californian
    born, or from the mid-west, or back east?
Maybe a recent immigrant? Does his family
    know where he is now? Did he break up
with someone he loved and fall into depression?
    Did he lose his job? What will he do tonight
for shelter? What about tomorrow and the day
    after tomorrow? He can't ask for handouts on
University Avenue, as the homeless used to do.

46

City ordinances in most Bay Area cities forbid
pan-handling. No disturbing shoppers along
    these tree lined streets. *"Tap, tap,"* the manager's
tapping the table. *"Order something or move on."*
    Peter waves as he parks his car across the street.

A LOS ANGELES SOLDIER IN IRAQ, AFGHANISTAN

I'm far from home in an unfamiliar country. How
    has this happened? Last month I was with
my family in LA. Now I'm on the other side
    of the world. Daydreaming of California,
wishing we could leave this country. Impossible.
    Our orders are *"to stay."* Tour duty extended,
redeployment common, whether we like it or not.
    How can we come close to the people here?
We're trained to: *"Stay on your guard! Don't trust
    anyone. Protect your buddies!"* I don't know
Arabic, not that I can get near the Iraqis to say
    anything. I enlisted in California's National
Guard to get a college education, not expecting
    I'd be sent outside America. Dawn rises over
the desert, similar to a summer morning in LA.
    Everything's hot and dry. Santa Ana winds
whip through the canyons. Back home December
    church bells are calling people to Mass, fiesta
of Madre de Guadalupe: I love the singing, dancing,
    delicious meals. Now I see men and women
putting everything aside, bowing towards Mecca
    as they pray to *"Allah."* I join my prayer to
theirs: *"Lord make me an instrument of your peace"*
    driving to the green zone with my buddies.

NEARBY SALEM, MASSACHUSETTS

During novitiate years close to the Topsfield,
    Massachusetts forest, I was ignorant of what
happened in nearby Salem at the beginning
    of our country, since we were isolated from
the world; so, after the convent, majoring in
    Political Science at Brooklyn College, I
studied New England settlements, (vividly
    portrayed by Arthur Miller's *"Crucible"*),
the witch hunts, prosecutorial obsessions,
    suspecting outsiders, prohibiting women
from becoming herbal healers, praising anyone
    who turned in family or friends to authorities,
punishing those who revealed governmental,
    religious, workplace secrets, ridiculing
dissenters, expelling undocumented immigrants,
    closing down *the Occupy movement,* preaching
human rights abroad as U.S. troops in Afghanistan
    carry on night raids in the homes of suspected
Taliban sympathizers, *surveillance* of our donations,
    keeping tabs on emails and web sites, though
brave folks still speak truth to those in power,
    standing beside the poor, persecuted, homeless,
the incarcerated, the unemployed, calling upon
    the example of Rosa Parks, Dorothy Day, Martin
Luther King Jr., Angela Davis, Daniel Ellsberg,
    Malcolm X, Daniel Berrigan and Maryknollers:
Ita Ford, Maura Clark, Lil Mattingly, Roy Bourgeois.

IN MEMORY OF DR. JOSEPH HENDERSON

You rub a dark smooth stone as you sit surrounded
    by Navajo sand paintings in your six-sided studio.
Native son of Nevada's Ruby mountains. Physician

advocating individuality, warning of *the collective's*
potential harm. Medicine healer melding Nature's
wisdom into down-to-earth kindnesses,
diagnosing shelter for introverts, direct light for
extroverts, brewing protection and bravery,
discerning differences, guiding men and women
through storms, working with their dreams and
ordinary challenges, prescribing painful separations,
or suggesting paths of reconciliation. You're
crossing your deck, a butterfly flits by as you turn
towards the studio opposite yours-- *"This was
my wife Helena's. She was a fine poet and dancer,
performing here on Sunday afternoons for family
and friends."* A redwood brushes your shoulders,
as you exclaim: *"Ah, the green tips of Spring on
this old growth giant."* I dare to ask: *"Are you afraid
of death?"* *"No, not at all. I hope dying will not be
difficult; otherwise, I'm looking forward to discovering
what it's like on the other side."* After tea, you insist
on walking me to the gate, where we wave goodbye.

MEETINGS WITH A REMARKABLE WOMAN,
NEW CAMALDOLI, BIG SUR, CALIFORNIA
for Thérèse Gagnon

White waves splashing continually over huge rocks
    below the monastery. Monks and retreatants

sing the *Salve Regina* around the Madonna and Child
    as the sun sets. A doe and faun nibble grass

inside the cloister garden. A family of quail dash across
    the path while I'm walking to the guest wing. I feel

warmth rising up my legs from wild wheat by the fence.
    A monk nods *goodnight* during *"Profound Silence."*

49

A blanket of fog rolls in first thing this morning; by noon
     the sun pushes through clouds, while Thérèse and I

relax on a bench overlooking the Pacific. *Catching up*
     after months apart. She is the reason I return. Her

presence essential to the community, as with her prayer
     shrines she creates in the forest, the rituals she

leads with guests, the fabulous French meals she makes.
     Such a contagious childlike spirit and abundant sense

of wonder. *"The Little Prince"* her typical spiritual reading
     at night near the Christmas lights she keeps up all

year long. How distill her essence in a potion to tuck in my
     pocket and carry home? Sun halo round her gray hair.

She waves to a fox trotting along the fence, bright stripes
     in dark red tail fur, eyes aglow, mischievous smile.

MIGRATIONS, IMMIGRATIONS

this time of year the monarch migrations along California's

coast   a steady stream southward   inner compass guide

stopping at Santa Cruz's Natural Bridges Park   wings

gently swaying   long clusters clinging to eucalyptus trees

orange and black spots pleated   a few stray ones caught

in fog   seeking safety of the fold   storing sap before

migrating south   to Central American forests   where they

were born   will mate   give birth   let go   fall to earth

offspring flying north   crossing the border   not stopped

for inspection -- though risky when friend Alma returns

to Mexico for her mother's funeral   will she be denied re-

entry to San Diego California   will she or her family be

incarcerated expelled as undocumented   our dear care-

givers   farm laborers   builders   cooks   gardeners   she

says   *"we did not cross the border, our people were here first,*

the border crossed over us."   I'm flying back east   a nonstop

from SFO to JFK   crossing over the central valley   Sierras

Rockies   Great Plains   *"bread basket of the world"*   mighty

magnificent Mississippi   silvery wing tipped plane banks

over the Atlantic's Riis Park beach where I swam ages ago

my heart's racing   table in upright position   thump of

wheels touch Queens   passengers clapping   bus ride

to my hometown   Brooklyn   no passbook needed

PERSISTENT PURITANISM, SALEM, MASSACHUSETTS

In the 1600's Salem, Massachusetts perpetrated
    the practice of executing women who were
condemned as witches. Some escaped death, so
    were banished to the wilderness, forced to
survive on their own. Preachers forbade herbal
    healing, prohibited dancing or singing. Any
suspects would be reported to the authorities.
    *"Worldly success signaled salvation. Poverty
a sign of God's displeasure."* Mistrust infiltrated
    every community. Remnants of this mentality
persist today-- consider hard-liners condemning
    the poor, banishing the undocumented they
label as *"aliens,"* while those on the opposite
    aisle may brag if their kids attend Ivy League
schools, if they rise in prestigious professions,
    "good ole spirit of independence, ingenuity, giftedness,"
the *MGM* program (Mentally Gifted Minors) changed
    its name to GATE (Gifted & Talented) . . . isn't
every child gifted and talented! . . . subtle powerful
    Puritanism equating *"the successful"* as best, so
unconsciously or deliberately blaming others for
    homelessness, poverty, while ignoring privileges
they, we, many enjoy early on, holding on to American
    "exceptionalism" at home and abroad, projecting evil,
bad intentions, selfishness outside oneself on to *"others"*

HESTER PRYNNE, SALEM, MASSACHUSETTS

    In Hawthorne's tale Hester Prynne is forced
by the Salem, Massachusetts townsfolk to sew
    a scarlet letter *"A"* on her blouse, a perpetual
humiliation, while the cowardly preacher kept
    his seduction secret, so never shared her fate.

52

NEW YORK CITY'S 42ND STREET LIBRARY

New York City's 42nd Street library's Berg Room
 displayed Eliot's manuscripts: *"The Waste Land,"*
"The Four Quartets" and *"Prufrock,"* when I was
 back east visiting my brother, who let me borrow
his old Buick, so I set out on a solo trip to Cape Ann,
 Massachusetts searching for remnants of Eliot's
"Dry Salvages." The car's windshield caught
 the sun off the Sound. Memories of my father
surfaced. I was a child, he held my hand as I waded
 in the pristine waters of Long Island across
the Sound at Sunken Meadow State beach and a final
 photo shows him waving a straw hat as he
strolls Orient Point beach near the home of friends
 who let him and my mother borrow their country
cabin. He loved all things near water and also
 this 42nd Street library, its stately lions flanking
the entrance, banners flapping over the façade,
 his Saturday haunt (if too cold for the beach),
a subway ride away from Flatbush, history books
 and LP records tucked under his arm. Today
my footsteps echo on the marble floor of the high
 ceiling entry hall. I'm heading to the Astor Room
for James Merrill's memorial service, tributes
 galore for his brilliant poetry, unparalleled
compassion to struggling unknown poets, as he
 offered me tea at his home not far from Central
Park, where as high school kids, Natalie and I
 got lost one night, while seeking the summer
Shakespearean festival; fortunately found by cops,
 who escorted us to the subway with a warning:
*"It's dangerous girls wandering at night in this
 section of the park."* We never dared return
for Shakespeare in the dark; neither did I discover
 "Dry Salvages" off Cape Ann, though I count

53

myself lucky to have viewed Eliot's manuscripts
    at the 42nd Street library; more profoundly
blest by JM's kind invitation to *"come over for tea."*

HOPKINS AND BRIDGES
"I want the one rapture of an inspiration."
    Gerard Manley Hopkins

Your friend's stingy praise. Such selfishness stings,
though you never say so. He's incapable of sympathizing
with your struggle year after year. He knows nothing of
being a writer without reassuring readers. His abundant
contacts in literature, yet he withholds a helping hand;
instead, self-defensiveness, self-promotion, though you try
banishing such thoughts. He dismisses your stanzas of
clouds, sunsets, birds, streams, storms, dreaming God's
grandeur as easy compositions. Yet you continually
encourage his work, while carrying on your ministries of
teaching, caring for the needy, struggling for writing time.
Self-doubts.   Silence.   Sickness.   Isolation.   Far from
home.   Laboring obscurely.   Inscape of rapture . . .

SØREN KIERKEGAARD

Your love for Regina became impossible. Far too
complicated to explain. She'd never understand why you
changed your plans. Some might say it was your father's
fault; his seriousness preventing you from becoming free
and easy-going. Whatever you decided was preceded by
a tortuous examination of conscience. Clouded skies,
dark paths, ravines through a forest of confusions that
opened and closed. Possibilities of marital bliss
went up in smoke. You knew well you'd never
make her happy. Setting Regina free, letting

her leave by breaking the engagement . . .
seeking God's compensatory presence
in everything you wrote.
                    A recluse silently
strolling the streets of Copenhagen, a brooding
young man dressed in dark clothes. People pointed
and wondered what was your occupation. Shocked
about your being the son of a minister, since you
rarely entered a church.
                    Facing your fears, doubts,
desires as if a Jacob wrestling with God's angel,
a Job weeping without loss of faith, a Magdalene
seeking Christ at the tomb.
                    You threw away
ready-made answers, man-made religious rules;
you leapt across the abyss believing God would
catch you in his arms, that reunion with Regina
was possible, so following Dante's example,
you endured the fires of purgatory and hell,
spiraling towards Bliss . . .
                    decades later
your intelligence dazzles, your restless spirit soars,
courage crowns your rejection of the crowd's pressure,
your non-conformity inspires daring . . .

IN MEMORY OF IRIS MURDOCH

Your vivid portrayals of human behavior
embedded in heavily philosophical novels;
    mischievous characters with alluring silly
charms, even in dire circumstances, affective
    conspiracies, masterfully drawing us
readers into seductive scenes of pleasurable
    suspense, as when the guy swimming
for his life in a raging stream was pulled
    into a deep ravine, till at the last minute

55

you tossed him on to a bright green slope
     and we heard him breathing heavily, sighing
with relief, since soon you offered an elixir
     of smoldering love in the ridiculous antics
of a seemingly mixed-matched couple falling
     for each other without a warning, their
awkward laughable gestures, testing each
     other's limitations; while another woman,
or is it a man, driven by jealous suspicion,
     shimmied up the balcony to spy on a couple
about to make love, so you wink, as it were,
     at us your readers, letting the secretive intruder
suddenly slip into a thorny rose bush, while
     across town a man is rummaging through
his wife's letters, determined to prove her
     unfaithful; yet most often your culprits
forgive and are forgiven, the way Mozart's
     characters do in his *Marriage of Figaro*.

RILKE'S "*MALTE*"

At a time when Europe was breaking apart
before World War I, the added pressures
of family expectations became unbearable.

Your mother waiting anxiously at the window
for your return. Prying questions, so privacy
became a matter of deceit. Your father a distant

formal figure. Neither offered encouraging
words. You carefully edited your days
to preserve independence, turning to poetry

for a refuge. Finally, you left home for someone
you would leave, having learned to master
another voice, writing as if you were a woman.

56

READING JAMES MERRILL,
INVERNESS, CALIFORNIA

Red-tail hawks glide through clouds over the green hills
of Marin. I'm taking a tangled trail above Tomales Bay

through an oak grove past redwoods and pines till path
swerves down to the pristine beach. Not a soul in sight.

Opening my knapsack, your poems fall on the damp
sand. Enchanted lines. Buried treasures. Cadences

with multiple meanings. Who hides in your stanzas?
Wit sprinkled wisely. Masterful shamanic language.

Estuary's multicolored jellyfish float under the footbridge.
Noisy shore birds skitter and scatter. Tiny muddy prints.

High tide, low tide streaks the sand. Chorus of concerns
evaporate, since I float along your buoyant stanzas.

Conjurer of Greece, the East coast, Vienna, Key West.
What will your readers do now that you are gone? Shall

I meditate on the undertow of vulnerability within your
courageous compassion. You befriended an unknown

poet. Perhaps religion played a role? My convent
background, your undisclosed diagnosis. A guessing

game. I read into your letters. Distracted by a heron's
low flying grace. Voices of children call in the cove round

the cliff. Blue jays disrupt my daydreams. I'm losing your
presence. Left to uncover buried maxims. Your last

note with the Arizona phone #, a way to call for your
birthday. If only I had phoned sooner. Such blessings:

your sunbursts of verbs, alluring adjectives, sweet asides,
powerful nouns, teasingly tender truths, strong humility.

THE LAWRENCE TREE, TAOS, NEW MEXICO
   for Joseph

On that hill where Lawrence lived while
composing "*Saint Mawr*" and other stories,
we were thrilled looking across the wide mesa.
Clouds gathered along the western ridge,
bolts of zigzagging lightning thrown through
thunder blasts near Los Alamos. No groundskeeper
sighted, so we dared do what we believed Lawrence
did with Frieda when they made love outdoors,
bringing each other to a fiery pitch, backs trembling
against this tree. Your brilliantly lit brown eyes
as the moon moved towards the sun behind your head.
Shafts of colorful rain began pouring into the Rio Grande.
Burnt-sienna body of the phoenix was glowing atop the altar
in DHL's white-washed chapel, wings flying over his ashes.

MERCURY/HERMES, INVERNESS, CALIFORNIA

Hail feathery creature flying through the terra-cotta ruins
of my heart, reviving your once-upon-a-time shrine. Shy,
bold, holding court with butterflies, scribes, astronomers,
sylvan creatures, laurels and willows. Your footsteps
on gravel beside the spring's liquid pulse. Inventing
summer trysts using broad strokes and vivid colors.
Arranging miniature roses round the border. Steaming
August streets. Champagne conversations. Incense

pleasuring the skirts of dancers. Tiny rainbow feathers
inside your ankles. Downy fluff on your shoulders.
Tipping your jaunty hat as you skip across the street . . .

PSYCHE AND EROS, INVERNESS, CALIFORNIA

A tall Herm stone is guarding a fork at the trail's crossroads

we're taking in the forest near Heart's Desire beach. You

carry a finely carved hiking stick, gift of your brother. I'm

reminded of Hermes' caduceus, symbol for healing. As we

cross the footbridge, bright orange jelly-fish ride high tide

into the green wetlands. While you're hiking to the ocean

I nap on warm sand, dreaming of Eros warning Aphrodite:

"Whatever you do, don't light the candle when I come to you at

night." Independent, incurably curious, Psyche lit the flame

causing Eros flight. Desperate for help, she pleaded with

Aphrodite, so assigned several tasks to prove her love for

Eros. *"Whatever you do, don't open Pandora's box, or you'll never*

see Eros again!" After completing her chores, Psyche fell

exhausted, and turned towards the tempting box, pried it

open, thus cast under its fatal spell, till Eros defied his

mother, flew to Psyche's side, brought a bouquet of healing

balms: *Star of Bethlehem* easing grief, *Red Chestnut* chasing

fear, *Olive's* strength, *Elm's* energy, *Gentian's* hope, so Psyche

rose refreshed, while I woke to warm breezes without

discerning the dream's significance till years later, after a

shattering loss, I was rescued by a grace-filled messenger's

insights, who said to me: *"There was a time I felt betrayed by*

God, when terrible things befell my family, since I had sacrificed

for their well-being. Months and years passed miserably, till it

finally dawned: God doesn't play favorites. Free agents all.

Forgive as you seek forgiveness. Love outlasts loss." Wasn't

I, weren't you, weren't we blest by wild flowered fields,

chartreuse seaweed by our feet, trail marked by manzanitas,

enchanting elms, comforting oaks, whistling pines, silvery

laurels, faithful redwoods and the familiar trail to the rustic

cabin, ah, grilled salmon, asparagus, brown rice by the fire,

making love surrounded by forest's night creatures calling . .

HELOISE AND ABELARD
for Joseph

Wild grasses, lavender and sunflowers fill
    the fields, where we've found a dilapidated
chapel, whose alcove offers shelter although
    its roof opens to the sky. A confessional
stall screens our lovemaking. Shattered
    stained glass fragments colorfully dot
the dirty floor. Song birds in the choir loft.
    No one knows our whereabouts, except
the kind messenger who secretly delivers
    our letters. Self-righteous judges posed
to punish us, if we're discovered. Tempting
    to carve our names in stone, yet we prefer
privacy. I treasure memories no one else
    can steal-- the way you swing your arms
when walking, your strong legs climbing trails,
    the scent of your sweaty clothes, smooth
skin of your inner wrists, sensitive hands
    and arms holding me close, rough beard
tickling my face, golden brown eyes laughing,
    the humming of your being inside me . . .

EXPECTATION, GOLDEN GATE PARK
for Madeline Grassi

A warm winter coaxed the catkins' furry
    tips into fresh blooms. Pacific breezes
rustle the cherry blossoms. Silvery aspen
    discs dance in the shade. School kids
follow a guide into the Fragrance Garden.
    Pink popcorn sold at the boathouse.
Turtles sunbathe on a large island rock.
    Paddleboats, bicyclists, waterfalls,

61

the Japanese pagoda, blue herons, the Botanical
    Garden, the Academy of Science, the de Young
Museum, the Rose Garden-- *"Who could ask*
    for anything more!" says a friend, while we
stroll through the Australian Rainforest before
    entering the Mediterranean garden. A few
months later, our son and daughter-in-law
    are beaming in the photo beside Stowe Lake--
taken the day they announced the baby's
    due date of early September. May Spring
bring us with the little one back to this park.

THOREAU

    His daily walk round Walden Pond,
then writing for hours, page after page,
    protesting war, urging citizens to refuse
paying taxes; he chose *"conscientious objector"*
    status as an alternative to military service.

THE 99% (of writers)

    Who dares defy the powers deciding who
gets published? No protests inside or outside
the board room. Is there a committee of one,
two, three or more, who *"know best"* what's
best to publish?
            MFA graduates, friends of
friends, insider's track? *"Thanks for supporting*
my cause. Definitely I'll read your manuscript."
Ah, the pressed palm, *"welcome aboard,"*
formal acceptance letter. *"Soon as you sign*
on the dotted line, our marketing campaign begins!"

"Everyone's equal in our eyes.
Excellence is everything. Exceptional craft
skills, lines of precision, dabs of skepticism,
punch-line at the end and yes, books we believe
will sell."
 "Our meetings aren't open to the public.
Sorry, keep on trying (elsewhere). Thanks for
thinking of us."
  "Redress? Repeal? Appeal? Sorry,
our decisions are final. Best to try another publisher.
Oh, on your way out, please close the door."

OH TIGRIS, OH EUPHRATES

Oh Tigris, Oh Euphrates watching Greek armies,
Roman archers, legionnaires armed to the teeth, British
forces, American military, empire building further, further
east and south crossing your deserts, mountains, ravines,
cities, villages, their shift shaping alliances, offensives,
insurgencies, crushing the centuries' old silk-trade routes,

Oh Tigris, descending Armenian highlands,
Oh Euphrates born in Kurdistan, watering earth's first
garden of Eden, marrying as one grand current seeping
through Basra emptying into the Persian Sea . . .

Oh Tigris, Oh Euphrates witnessing the Greeks, Romans,
British, Americans' sighting enemies over the next ridge,
ever expanding military exploits taking a toll on men,
women, children, plants, animals, Nature, here and at
home: the homeless, the unemployed, the sick, orphans,
widows, the aged, the rich richer, the poor poorer . . .

Oh Tigris, Oh Euphrates seeing generations of generals
crossing your sacred shores, their unquenchable thirst for

wealth, power, influence, aiming to outdo other occupiers,
not forgetting Alexander's legendary exploits inside Persia

Oh Tigris, Oh Euphrates birthing Babylonian, Persian,
Shiite, Sunni, Kurdish communities beside your endlessly
flowing waters, while Greeks, Romans, British, Americans
stole artifacts, resources, strategically set at crossroads
of civilization, *Oh Tigris, Oh Euphrates* . . .

DISCRIMINATION
in memory of my mother, Bertille Ball Cook

Near the end of her life, my mother
needed a nursing home, so I was given
a *"grand tour"* of several facilities,
then the inevitable cold shoulder *"No,"*
once they learned Mom was on *Medi-Cal.*

RIO DEL MAR, APTOS, CALIFORNIA

Was it yesterday, we were choosing this
Rio del Mar home for our family, the fresh air
for our sons Eddie and Peter, the hiking trails,
redwoods, open space and near a public school.

Our living room overlooked Monterey Bay.
You built the back staircase for Mom's private
entrance beside the garden we planted with chard,
lettuce, carrots, onions plucked by a gopher. until
our cat Gypsy dared to chase away the creature.

Sumner Avenue's unmarked trail *"our secret
passageway."* The boys always running ahead
under an old Pacific Lumber company train trestle,
passing through a pine grove, surrounded by
raspberry brambles, ferns and poison oak till

64

the trail's rickety make-shift stairs, we'd jump
on stones across a creek, landing on damp sand
of the wide deserted beach whose wild capped
waves greeted us as we gazed south towards
Moss Landing, Monterrey and across the Bay
at the dark green silhouette of Pacific Grove,
the white sandy coast of Carmel; then north to
Seacliff's concrete ship, Capitola's pier, Twin
Lakes harbor, the Santa Cruz boardwalk, faint
outline of Lighthouse Point, a favorite haven
for surfers, windy West Cliff Drive to Natural
Bridges State beach and its eucalyptus grove,
migratory home for monarch butterflies.

We always took the dirt road back, since
the boys liked sighting rabbits popping up,
vanishing into underground warrens. (That
was the year we read *"Watership Down."*)

Now, after you've passed over, I'm standing
with Eddie before our once-upon-a-time home.
His kids, my grandkids, Madeline and Ethan,
are watching us cry. *"Sometimes people cry when
they remember happy times and we miss grandpa."*

Heading back to the freeway, the familiar twists,
turns, bumps, stops of Pebble Beach Drive, Pinehurst
Drive, Club House Drive. I'm recalling your commute
to Santa Clara University, why we left Rio del Mar. Not
worth the risk over 17. I was nearly killed in a head-on
collision on a back road from Soquel to the Summit,
planning to meet you at a presentation by our friend,
Father Tenny Wright; instead 13 stitches in the ER
at Dominican Hospital.

A thick fog blankets the freeway, till a golden light
swirls in a circle over Santa Cruz, a *Paradiso* moment,
this tangible sense of your *nearness* as I merge on
to 17, passing Scotts Valley's Mount Hermon Road
leading to Felton's Henry Cowell Redwood State Park,
Route 9 to our once-upon-a-time Ben Lomond cabin
built entirely by you after we moved back to the valley.
(Unfortunately an *El Niño* storm washed out the road.
Too costly for us to maintain, so we sold to an enthusiastic
young couple, eager to take on the challenges of *Nature*.)

Now solo, I'm coasting over the summit, sudden
downhill curves, round and round till the opening
stretch alongside Lexington Reservoir above Los Gatos,
into that *aha* moment-- seeing the Santa Clara valley
spread below, redwoods, cedars, palms, pines, sweet gum
trees, pockets of plum orchards, San Jose skyscrapers,
Mission Santa Clara, suburban sprawl blurring boundaries
between Los Gatos, Campbell, Cupertino, Sunnyvale,
Mountain View, Palo Alto, San Mateo, Burlingame,
Millbrae, San Bruno, Pacifica, Daly City, San Francisco,
and to the northeast: Milpitas, Fremont, Castro Valley,
Oakland, Berkeley and beyond . . . once-upon-a-time
Land of milk and honey, almond and plum orchards,
before the high tech revolution . . . HP, Atari, Apple,
Google, Facebook, Sun Microsystems, Advanced
Micro Devices, Cisco Systems, Netflix, so forth
and so on rippling across city, county, state, country,
globe, name-altering, game-changing, *Silicon Valley.*

SMOLDERING ASHES, INVERNESS, CALIFORNIA
in memory of Joseph Grassi

a thick green forest
                    trail backlit by
                                      sun through fog

memory's potent residue
                  since you've passed
                                  through
death's door
        after an unexpected storm
                            almost tore us apart
we crossed the footbridge
                holding each other close
overseeing golden jellyfish
                riding a see-through stream
inland marshes
            quaking aspens
                    brambles   ferns
oaks   pines
          blackberry bushes
                  red-tailed hawks spiraling
warm thermals
           herons over Tomales Bay
                      we follow
the twisting trail
          through the woods
                  to a rented rustic cabin
San Andreas fault line's nearby
                unexpected aftershocks
my unsteady sense
            of self after you've
                  passed over
I've lost my inner compass
             I seek the cabin again
                    sad to
hear the kind owner
           has also departed
                I see redwoods
piercing clouds
           surviving droughts
                Nature's abiding

67

gentle giants swaying in song
                              overseeing our fault lines
not judging how high
                    our mistakes
                                all forgiven
I turn to take your hand
                        gone   you've   gone
                                          beyond
the blue horizon   wind   sun   stars   night   day
                                          back
to our beginnings
                      discovering   a pair of mollusks
found cleaving to
                    a burnt-sienna cliff
                                    that we scaled
ever adventurous a couple   hearts and
                                souls seeking
Nature's green shoots
                      of hope trail appearing through
a fallen oak
            as you spoke of how
                              death was composting life
ever words of wonder
                    now nesting in my being
                                          along
with your practical Latin aphorisms
                              making me laugh
strong steady seeking new trails
                              affection outlasts
loss   a bow to Divine Nature
                        grafting our hearts and souls
as a burning hearth
                  bringing loved ones into
                                    the world
smoldering ashes   multiple generations of
                                    Allelulias

V

COLERIDGE

"As a man or woman treat themselves, so God treats us;
Who waits the asking when they see the need,
In their mean heart goes half-way to refuse;
Whereas, God companions us on our way,
And this he does unasked . , ."
Dante, *Purgatorio, Canto XVII*

"Some hope their neighbor's ruin may divert
His glory to themselves, and this sole hope
Prompts them to drag his greatness down . . ."
Dante, *Purgatorio, Canto XVII*

"It has been said of Coleridge that for him at all stages
of development politics and religion were inseparable.
That is equally true of Dante."
Dorothy Sayers, translator of Dante's *Divine Comedy*

COLERIDGE AND WORDSWORTH

"What if the mind were a thousand times
more beautiful than the earth"-- Wordsworth.
"What if stars sparkle and planets glide not only over
seas and shores, but also inside our deeds and desires"
-- Coleridge

Fast friends from the first, not to the last . .
    Coleridge and Wordsworth, side by side,
hiking British and Scottish mountains, forests,
    fields, moorlands, warming themselves
beside midnight fires, conversations lasting
    for hours, sharing friendships with Dorothy,
Mary and Sara; while Wordsworth populated
    his poetry with lyrical Lake District legends,
childhood memories, Oxford years and tranquil
    romantic Nature musings, while Coleridge
shaped strangely supernatural poems, sprinkled
    with misty mountains, desolate caves, stormy
seas, turbulent landscapes, an albatross, a mariner,
    ghosts, goddesses, nightmares, guilt, rejection.
Was Wordsworth worried whether Coleridge
    was coming too close to the women they both
loved? Did Coleridge feel betrayed by Wordsworth
    rejecting his nature poems from their collaborative
book? Coleridge left for Malta. Friendship severed.
    Years later, they were invited to the London home
of a mutual friend. Wordsworth presided over
    the dinner conversation, while the ordinarily
loquacious Coleridge stayed silent and left early;
    spending his last years in relative obscurity
at the residence of a caring physician friend; unlike
    Wordsworth courted in old age by followers
at his Lake district Rydal estate in the company of
    the women whom Coleridge also dearly loved.

WILLIAM'S WORDS

For several months I've suppressed what
    I sensed at the start: he craved fame
and needed a wife, children, his sister,

sister-in-law, friends and an adoring
    public. He used my poems as fodder
for his writings. You think I'm wrong, but

you don't know how I was mistreated.
    You've not overheard our conversations,
personal confidences, plans for publishing

together; then his change of mind after
    my editing was completed. He struck
my poems from *our pages*, implying they

weren't worthy of inclusion. It's embarrassing
    saying these things, but you asked about
my relationship with William. Yes, he

assigned me *the supernatural theme,* yet
    rejected my *"Christabel,"* believing
his *nature poems* were best, although

I wrote on *nature* first and he followed
    suit! Why do I bother being his friend?
Does my affection resemble a wisteria vine

attached to a familiar wall? I should follow
    the way animals flee their shelter if they
feel threatened. You're right: I've been

betrayed. It's unrealistic to think he will
    change. I was wrong to trust him.

I'll sail far from England. Poetry must become

my refuge. I'll try to forget our friendship
      and recall Dorothy, Mary and Sara,
who know me better than William ever will.

COLERIDGE'S CONFLICT

I labored several weeks over the poem before
      carrying "*Christabel*" for fifteen miles to
William's Dove Cottage, where I expected
      an enthusiastic approval since he *assigned* me
the supernatural theme, while keeping Nature
      for himself. Were my hands shaking as I
handed him the pages? Dorothy, Mary and Sara
      were waiting with me for his words, shocked
to hear: "*Revise it.*" So retracing my steps
      through heavy storms tearing across
slippery mountain slopes, down dangerous
      ravines, lashing across the lake, at last
home in Keswick, spending hours revising
      the poem, plagued by arthritis, nightmares,
self-doubt, isolation. Once again I'm carrying
      "*Christabel*" to William. He apologizes, yet
stays firm, refusing a share in the fame he is
      carefully orchestrating behind the scenes.
Defensive if I question his lack of generosity.
      His unwavering self-assurance. Am I losing
my self-confidence by continuing close to him?

WILLIAM'S WISHES

While we were standing beside a waterfall in
      the woods below William's home, golden
sycamore leaves brushed your hair. Twigs
      were tickling your bare arms. Shafts of sun-

72

light pierced the shadowy forest floor. Foxes
        trotted in the underbrush. Sparrows flitting
tree to tree. A mother quail sheltering little ones
        inside a hollow log. Close enough to hear your
labored breathing, as we climbed the slippery
        slope. He was waiting impatiently at the top
for your return. I feared losing you. His subtle
        persuasive powers. At the gate you turned,
waving goodbye before following William within.

DRY DOCK

Wild winds tear away the golden maple leaves
        of late October, as we carry the boat up

the embankment. Flipping it over, lowering
        it carefully onto wooden stilts, since winter

is near. Tiny grey barnacles adhere. Yellowish
        green algae rippling along its spine. Tufts

of dried daffodils fall from the seat. Relics of
        past outings. We toss a blue tarp overhead,

watching it fill with air, so land like a parachute
        blanketing the boat. One by one taking turns

we thread the silky damp rope through metal
        hoops for fastening the tarp tightly. Protection

is crucial. Something sharp cuts my hand. A line
        of blood trickles down my wrist. He stops

his task and asks if I'll be joining Mary, Dorothy
        and him at dinner, or am I planning to

73

head home? A blast of chilling wind hits me
　　full force, perhaps a warning if I should outstay

my welcome. Best for everyone if I pack my bags
　　tonight. Feigning regret, he'll ask me to stay,

while I know he hopes I leave, allowing him
　　a solo performance for this exclusive audience.

SAILING WITH WILLIAM

I was putting away our breakfast things when he
said: *"It'll be our last chance to sail before winter."*

Crisp Autumn air. Bare gray branches of an old
hickory kept scratching the roof. We pushed open

the back door. Tiny thorns of raspberry bushes
scratched my legs. Down the trail to the pier,

where the dingy waited. We rowed to the sailboat.
Once aboard, tacking towards the islands. Groves

of bright red and golden maples were waving along
the shore. We darted every which way, mirroring

my confusion. Clouds rose ominously. My heart
was racing. Wanting to act persuasively, but lacking

the skill. What good were my poems if they failed to
empower me in the *real world*? What should I do

to save my self-respect? Poetry's my calling. Where's
a guide at the crossroads? Why continue this illusion

of friendship, when he pretends generosity, as he privately
grabs for the spotlight? Our last sail together: rain storm

pelted us full force. I thought we'd capsize, drown.
Luckily we reached shore. I stayed up late writing him

a farewell letter before leaving for the city. He is content
in the cocoon of women, who are devoted to his writing.

DOROTHY'S DILEMMA

Why am I afraid to speak honestly? I've longed to
hike alone with him in the woods, yet fear William's
      anger if I come too close to Coleridge. Three of us
sailed to Germany. My hopes rose and fell with each
      approaching wave, as I imagined weeks of hiking
together, staying overnight at country inns, writing
      side by side in the light of a fire, reading our work
to each other. After the ship docked, William aborted
      our plans, telling Coleridge it was best if he headed
north to Lübeck, while we'd leave for southern Germany.
      Such an agony for me when we were apart, waiting
for a letter. Did I, do I, love him as more than a friend?
      Am I deceiving myself, believing he will reciprocate
my affection? William's ridiculous if he thinks I'd run
      away with a married man. Such a scandal. It's true,
in the end, I'll do what I always do, doing whatever
      my brother wishes. Oh, the brilliance of Coleridge's
mind, a sun bursting through clouds, such wildly
      expressive eyes, intense beliefs banishing boredom,
his vulnerable health calling for compassion, his
      thrilling voice penetrating my daydreams, magical
cadences of his conversation, his mesmerizing glace
      startling me to the core. Back in England hiking
on the moors with him and William, by the fireside

sharing poetry, philosophy, nature, politics. Sensitive
to his moods, I respond as a flower does to the wings
of a pollinating bee, so store his essence as an elixir
inside the honey hive of my secret self. No one has or
will come as close, not even William, who relies on
my sisterly affection, for whom I take dictation and nurse
him through sicknesses, ever encouraging his poetry,
recalling our Cumberland childhood, *on call* for his
and Mary's children, a sister, sister-in-law, an aunt
serving their needs. Sometimes at night, I whisper
the name of the one I love: *Samuel . . . Samuel . . .*

SARA'S WONDERING .   .   .

I'm wondering if things might have been different--

if I had expressed my feelings? Fear of offending

others fanned my caution. After he left, there was no

forwarding address, no news if or when he would

return. Were there regrets? My tendency to chastise

myself if I should place my needs before that of others.

Was there *a message* I missed when he burst into

the cottage that stormy night, or was he simply saying

goodbye to everyone? A wild look in his eyes, hair wet

and tangled, boots muddied by hiking the mountains.

We sipped brandy by the fireside. He left before dawn.

SARA'S LOSS

By midnight the pines were thick with icicles.
    Next morning, the gray cottage was freezing
    and the fields blanketed by snow. Mountain

tops shimmered. Your note under the door: *"Don't*
    worry when I'm away. I'll be fine. So will you."
    Harsh winds scattered the elm and maple leaves.

A squirrel's nest clung tenaciously to a high hickory.
    Rays of weakened winter light pierced the forest
    floor. Harbor emptied of boats. Hawks were

careening wildly. After breakfast I walked the shore
    alone, found golden threads of water sparkling
    by the muddy path turning to ice. Later at lunch

the embers of our last night's fire were smoldering
    behind the grate. Proof of your presence in my
    famished memory. Was it a dream or an illusion?

Less than 24 hours ago we were enjoying panfried fish
    and garden vegetables. Before someone unseen
    called you away. Swallow nests under the eaves.

Is that you at the back door? No, just blasts of cold
    wind from the west. I pulled the potted plants
    indoors to save from frost. You've left the country

for an unknown destination. Who knows if, or when,
    you'll return? I'm sipping tea as I read your letters.
    Steam veils the window. Your words inside me . . .

BON VOYAGE

Who knows when we'll meet again. I'll always
remember you framed by the doorway of the cottage.
    Sheets of rain blowing behind your back. You
possessed the wild look of a man weathering a storm
    alone. I wanted to dry you with a towel and make
a bed beside the fire. I didn't realize you'd be leaving
    for months, or more. Perhaps I sensed that possibility.
A bundle of books tied by a rope were tossed over
    your shoulder. *"Come in, rest." "I can't. I need to
say goodbye."* Why suddenly? Where are you going?
    What has lured you away? Tenderness in your voice.
*"No matter what happens, I know you'll be the one to
    forgive me."* A compliment or consolation prize
making me smile. Believing against all odds our love
    will endure everything; I'll wait with open arms.

AFTER HE'S GONE

Hiking home through blazing Fall foliage,
    I'm slipping on uneven stones and struggling
over boulders. Forcing myself not to turn back.
    Comforting courageous mountains, strong
vulnerable valleys, protective forest mantel,
    wild roses in the fields, lacy lichen covering
stone walls. Lambs' wool on fences. Orange berries
    brighten dark green hedges. Clouds mysteriously
gather. There is so much I do not know and will
    never know. Love's a leap of faith across the dark
divide. Heading home under watchful eyes of red-
    tailed hawks. Seagulls seeking the shore. Eagles
soaring over cliffs. Crickets in crevices. A smoldering
    sense of loss. A rowboat reaches the island, where

we hiked this summer. Bees cover the clover. Honey
hives, preserves, warm scones. Love's hibernating
pleasures. Our innocence endangered by poachers, who
hid behind our backs. Defending ourselves against
intruders. Embers of yesterday's fireside in our
hearts. Desire resurrected at dawn. Life's an open
book, where I pen your presence in indelible ink.

VI

DONATELLO

"I know the embers of the ancient flame."
Dante, *Purgatorio, Canto XXX*

"Make strong my tongue that in its words may burn
One single spark of all Thy glory's light
For future generations to discern   .   .   ."
Dante, *Paradiso, Canto VII*

"When proper respect towards the dead is shown at
the End and continued after they are far away, then
the moral force of a people has reached its highest point."
Confucius, *The Analects*

DONATELLO'S CHRIST WITH ANGELS

1.

While wandering through unfamiliar rooms
    in the Victoria and Albert Museum,
we come suddenly upon a life-sized figure
    of Christ sleeping in the arms of two little
angels. Will he wake if we kiss his hands?
    Should I try mouth to mouth resuscitation
that I learned as a lifeguard? Will an alarm
    alert the guards? Are the angels whispering
encouraging words in his ears? Will a rainbow
    appear if they carry him in a fiery chariot?

2.

As the little angels lift you, their feathers slip
    between your fingers. I'm close enough to kiss
your lips. Your head's bowed, chest slackened,
    yet such strength in your shoulders. Soldiers
tortured you, though the scars are camouflaged,
    so you appear beautifully serene, yet vulnerable.

3.

I long to anoint your body, trace the veins visible
    below your translucent skin and caress the fine
bones forming your face. If only it were possible
    to erase the shadows under your eyes, place
lavender and poppies beside your arms and legs,
    wrap a linen shroud around you. A guard's
shouting: *"No touching! You'll set off the alarm!"*

4.

I fell in love with your smile, gentle eyes, the sound
    of your voice, charismatic intelligence, down-to-
earth practicality; other dear details swirling in
    my memory since you've passed over and now
I struggle with doubts of the afterlife mixing with
    hope for reunion, as I seek you *in all the old
familiar places* near home and far away. *Is that you
    walking through a grove of redwoods?* Remember
our vowing love *"till death do us part"* and beyond . . .

5.

Some say he is more beautiful than any god
    shaped by human hands: this Christ asleep
in a city far from where he was born. Now
    vulnerable, unclothed. Friends are far away.
Strangers seized him, yet Donatello often kept
    vigil from dawn to dusk. Did anyone console
him after such a loss? Or was he left to grieve alone?

6.

You said nothing can separate us; yet you are
    more spiritual than I, believing in the unseen
life, while I'm more attached to the sensual here
    and now. After you disappeared, we met again
in the garden. *"No. Not now."* when I tried to
    touch you. *"Soon, we'll be reunited. Do not feel
rejected; savor my presence humming within your
    being, our love encoded the way fingerprints are
endemic to identity."* Do I take your love on faith?
    Do you take mine for granted; or am I mixing
us up? I confess to having loved you at first sight.

7.

Were friends indifferent to his work or supportive,
    letting him know they realized how hard it was
laboring alone in summer heat and freezing winter?
    Was he plagued by self-doubt, or simply content,
believing his creativity was *a calling*. At night he often
    dreamed of the one who waited in his studio.
Some say he wept after completing this body of Christ.

8.

They say you were imprisoned, brutally
    tortured, then painfully executed;
yet here you are as if serenely asleep.
    Looking closer, I find the wounds
in your hands, feet and chest. I touch
    your forehead, where they forced
a crown of thorns; these hidden sites
    of torture in your beautiful body.

9.

On entering the dark forest, did Dante fear
    what was beyond the bend in the road,
or was he confident Beatrice would appear,
    as in Florence, when he was nine years old
and she gazed into his eyes, searing his soul,
    so years later, he believed she'd rescue him
from purgatory and hell, drawing him towards
    the folds of a gorgeous luminous rose in
her heavenly home; perhaps prefiguring these
    adoring angels who lift this lovely Christ.

10.

Late last night, I reluctantly left my studio;
    rushing first thing this morning to greet
these alert angels, who kept watch, while
    I was resting. Now I wash my hands,
bend over the table, whisper affectionately
    in his ear, choose the tools for transforming
earthy marble into the One I adore and in
    doing so, dare believe I possess powers
peculiar to priests capable of changing
    ordinary things into his *real presence*.

11.

Mercury's silvery wings, Eros's adoring
    arrow, Apollo's sun-drenched chariot,
Daphne's graceful flight, Pan's mischievous
    melodies, Orpheus's enchanting songs,
Eurydice's heart-breaking fall, Psyche's
    remarkable resurrection, Aphrodite's
April allure, Demeter and Persephone's
    marvelous reunion, Gabriel's daring
proposal, Mary's courageous consent,
    Christ's wintry arrival, Dante's pursuit
of Beatrice, Donatello's incarnational art.

12.

A pair of angels shelter this adorable
    man.   His life pulse is fading. Hands
of a healer now still. Translucent skin,
    delicate veins, strong arms, muscular

shoulders. No visible wounds, yet he was
    tortured, jailed and executed. Possibly
art's protest against the death-penalty . . .

13.

My heart was racing when I realized you
    were taken away. Who will help me
rescue you? Will angels of mercy arrive
    out of the blue and counsel patience?
My doubts and fears fly round the room.
    Will you return as a man from the land
of the dead? I'll rub your body with lavender
    and almond oils. We'll laugh and sleep
in each other's arms, humming *Alleluias.*

14.

Guide me through this dark forest of doubt,
    since my loved one's passed over and I
long for his presence. Rekindle my heart's
    hope. Light the fires of memory buried
in ashes. Allow comforting angels to weep
    with me and wring their tiny fists the way
they do in a Giotto fresco, when Christ
    died, while awaiting the winged chariot
descending from clouds to carry him home.

15.

Loving the legends and lineage of Greek
    and Roman gods, he recalled Hermes,
winged healer at the crossroads, Eros
    aiming affectionate arrows across
the abyss, Apollo's dawn shining into
    dark despair, Pan's playful tunes
echoing in the forest, Baucus weaving
    grapes vines and laurel leaves into
crowns, Neptune frolicking with nymphs;
    Donatello chiseling these disappearing
spirits into his adorable Christ with angels.

16.

I long to midwife my loved one's passage,
    support his shoulders, as these little
angels lift their adorable Christ, stroking
    his forehead, whispering in his ears:
"You're almost home," coaching him across
    the great divide, while their hearts
are breaking, since they must let him go . . .

17.

I hear the twin angels breathing nearby.
    A clock's ticking in the gallery, or is it
our hearts beating loudly? The little one
    on the right looks hopeful, the other angel
appears doubtful, as they hold Christ close
    in their arms, fingers woven in feathers;
perhaps both wonder what to do next?

18.

Are you asleep, departed, deceased?
    Will I ever hear your voice again?
They are lifting your arms over their
    shoulders. I implore, as if they
possess the power to raise you from
    the dead. I kiss your head, chest
and hands, caress your wrists, anoint
    your feet with oil. My camera's flash
destroys the spell you cast. Shadows
    bleed round the edges of the room.
Footsteps in the hallway. Not enough
    time to say goodbye, as I had hoped.

19.

His radiant intelligence, sensitive nature
    and devotion to making life better for
others. Many grieved his disappearance.
    Only a miracle can bring him back. If
he wakes, will I be near enough to help
    heal his wounds, listen to his story,
promise him he will never be forgotten.

20.

Magdalene pushed through the crowd
    surrounding him and touched his arm.
Someone shouted for her to stop! They
    spread stories destroying her reputation,
begging him to cast her off, but she knew
    no one could destroy their love, even if
he was taken away, hidden far from home;
    she never gave up hope of his return,
no matter what others said behind her back.

21.

They were walking by the Sea of Galilee,
    olive groves lining the hills, almond
blossoms covering the valley, plane trees
    forming an arch over the fountain just
past the temple gate. He found a sundial
    in the lavender garden and showed her
how its reassuring warmth swings round
    after storms. His hands rested near hers
on the ledge. Atmosphere charged with
    anticipation. They left the cloister, as
a couple, seeking a new life in the world.

CARAVAGGIO'S "LAMENTATION"

Your soft red chalk caresses his vulnerability
shaping the chamber music of desire and grief,
though understanding evaporates every time
I remember he vanished. His luminous skin
preserved in the strong tones you suggest,
maybe meaning you were weeping through
brush strokes while painting, since he left
without a goodbye note. Burnt offerings,
prayer flags. Why apologize for tears,
after all you can't help seeking God's
presence here and there on earth   .   .   .
so your magical red caulk is lifting
his body from the dusty background of
this canvass, weaving four tiny angels' feathers
within his fingers; they're calling him back
to life, heart beating loudly within this chamber.

GIOTTO'S ARENA CHAPEL, PADUA

I pray these tiny angels' primitive wings will
never cease beating every whichway round his
shoulders. Giotto's Christ painted in primary
colors and undisguised emotions. Scenes carefully
scented by lilies, roses, violets, lavender, engraved by
kisses, stained by grief. Clouds parting, the curtain is torn
in two. I'm joining these melancholy angels as I wrap
a favorite blanket round your body, light candles, kiss
your hands, feet, forehead, lips, seeking comfort from
this portrayal of life after death saturated by beauty
and pathos, joy and tears everywhere I wander within
this magical chapel beloved by countless visitors.

CONSOLATION PRIZE, FRA LIPPI

Did you see Him down by the riverside? Did He
leave His heart in your town too? Ah, this pale blue

breath-takingly beautiful painting that's brightened
by gold round the border; a consolation prize for us

doubters, who persist nevertheless in pursuing faith,
no matter the consequences, taking comfort in Fra

Lippi's sympathetic portrayal of Christ's mother
sitting beside angels smiling through tears.

ONCE-UPON-A-TIME

Once-upon-a-time long, long ago in a land far, far away,
    a woman named Miriam was reading sacred texts,
when thunder roared and lightning flashed through
    the open doorway of her home. The wind whistled
loudly as a luminous creature flew into the room and
    Miriam felt afraid, yet bravely came close and dared
to touch the downy tips of the creature's golden wings:
*"Greetings Miriam, I'm Gabriel, who's come to ask: if
you will carry God's special message of love into the world?"*
    "Yes, yes, but why me?" A smile crossed the angel's
face as he leapt high, landing on tiptoe, opening
    his arms wide as Miriam joined in the dance. They
began singing: *"All we are asking is give peace a chance."*
    Suddenly they stopped as silence filled the room,
then the angel's gold and scarlet robe started stirring.
    The blue sash across his chest tightened. A strong
wind blew his black hair. His wings began beating,
    picking up speed, fast, faster. Miriam shouted:
*"Don't leave. Who'll believe me?" "Don't worry. All
will be well."* As if a shooting star, Gabriel flew
into the clouds, leaving silvery footprints and a few
    tiny feathers on the floor. Eventually Miriam told
her fiancée Joseph about the angel's visit. He promised
    his protection. They married at Passover. So it came
to pass: she gave birth to a beautiful baby whom they
    named: *"Noel, God with us."* Sometimes she doubted
what had happened, or feared the future, until she
    held the feathers close to her heart. This tale of
Miriam and the angel's visit is told in various versions
    over many years among peoples in lands near and far.

DOVE DESCENDING IN SONG

Yes,
beautiful
ordinary creatures
inhabiting divine forms
thanks to artful songs opening
the heart space of our longing, distilling
an elixir of hope into drops of honey I mix
in jasmine tea, since needing all the help I can get
after my precious love has passed over, so I'm recalling
ordinary resurrections as those tiny pink buds bursting in
bloom on the Japanese maple tree in our garden and green
fuzzy capes sheltering blond almonds in our back yard
plus dear sundial spinning on dark wintry afternoons
by my beloved's hands in San Jose's Municipal Rose
Garden down the street from our home and now
a sheen of frost melts in Prospect Park's great
meadow before we moved out west where
forget-me-nots and roses were welcoming
us to Madre de Guadalupe's Santa Clara
Mission shrine, her Dove's descending
in my kitchen as Leonard Cohen's
lyrics swirl round my cooking
his amazing *Hallelujah!*
Hallelujah! Hallelujah!

VII

SANCTUARY

"   .   .   .   is it possible that what some resent in Dante
is not his suffering but his serenity,
not the nostalgia but his triumphant coming-home."
Dorothy Sayers, translator of Dante

"   .   .   .   Oh joy no tongue can tell
Oh wealth past want, that never shall fade or fly"
Dante, *Paradiso, Canto XXVII*

"Ring the bells that still can ring,
Forget your perfect offering,
There is a crack, a crack in everything,
That's how the Light gets in,
That's how the Light gets in   .   .   ."
Anthem, Leonard Cohen

POINT REYES PENINSULA, CALIFORNIA
in memory of my mother, Bertille Ball Cook

My mother would have loved Inverness's
Heart's Desire beach along with the beautiful
    Point Reyes National seashore; she never
lost her childlike sense of awe on arriving
    in California . . . Santa Clara was *"paradise,"*
the sky over the Santa Cruz mountains always
    "spectacular," an occasional complaint during
a heat wave: *"the sun's so hot in California!"* perhaps
    the way Woody Allen felt in his film *"Annie*
Hall" fleeing Hollywood fast as possible back
    to his beloved New York, Mom's hometown
too, though she fell in love with everything
    Californian and never wanted to leave   . . .
By the time Joe and I found Point Reyes,
    Mom was unable to travel far by car, so
I've imagined she is with me, loving the lupine,
    wild irises, oak groves, pines, laurels, ferns,
redwoods, berry bushes and golden marshes
    swaying by the shore near the forest's edge,
where we step into the calm waters of Tomales
    Bay, seaweed tickling our toes, swimming
side by side, gazing at the misty Marin hills
    (resembling grandma's Scottish highlands),
breaststroke to the raft, resting on warm planks
    bobbing up and down under bursts of sun-
light, fleeting fog, hawks circling within thermal
    currents, kids laughing in the cove, wide
wings of a blue heron swish over us, downy
    feathers fluttering, as we hum the hymn
sung in our Brooklyn Flatbush parish: *"Come*
    Spirit, comforter creator blest, and in our hearts
take up your rest. Come with your grace and
    heavenly aid to heal the hearts that you made . . ."

MATER DOLOROSA BY LORENZO LOTTO

Such a forlorn look in the mother's eyes,
        as if she knew her consent to conceive
meant someday her child would be at risk,
        likely leave home on reaching maturity
and not look back. Perhaps shrug his shoulders
        at her devotion and expect a *Yes* to whatever
he plans. Or he may share his journey joyfully
        with her throughout his life. I think it is
the painter, Lotto, who is projecting the future
        here. He gives her smile a tinge of sadness,
portrays her as young, yet not a carefree youth,
        applies creases of worry round her eyes and
hints at her possessing a keen intuition, as if she
        knows the future and accepts all in advance
for reasons beyond our fathoming. She is letting
        her baby play with the pomegranate. An old
man waves a palm that provides shelter from
        the sun. Who knows whether she wonders
if he will follow his father's wishes, no matter
        the danger. Will she be consulted, offer
advice? A yellow mantel covers both mother
        and child, silvery threads woven in their blue
hemlines. Holding him close, she hums a lullaby.

SKIPPING STONES, LAKE HOPATCONG, NJ
in memory of my father, Edwin A. Cook

An August sun sets on Lake Hopatcong, New Jersey,
        as Dad is showing Richie, John and me how to
throw smooth stones sideways so they skip over

the silent waters. I kneel on the still warm sand,
        studying his swift graceful arcs the way he swims
in the Atlantic beyond the jetties of Riis Park beach.

Wavelets tickle my fingers. I'm fishing for a flat stone.
    This *scene* may be from the summer before I waved
goodbye to my family at the convent door, vanishing

into a world they'd never know, brief glimpses on formal
    visiting days. Learning the rules: "*No talking in twos.*"
Confined to speaking only at set times in certain places,

more freedom on feast days as Christmas, Easter
    and Pentecost. Evening's *Profound Silence* broken
by a sister ringing a bell at dawn, our sleepy response:

"*Benedicamus Domino!*" chorus of: "*Deo Gratias!*"
    Daily rituals undisturbed the smooth surface of
convent life, unlike the trumpet call at summer camp

rousing us city girls from rest hour, so we'd jump down
    the cabin steps, skip over stones across the stream,
aim a bow and arrow at an archery target, take turns

lugging a large steel milk container, heavy as a boulder,
    for an overnight on Mount Zorn, join in a circle of
rowboats at day's end, our songs rising over Silver Lake.

Singing a peaceful Taps over the valley. Decades later
    shattering a convent silence: phone call about Dad's
surgery; so Richie drove me to the hospital that night

before Dad died. No grief counseling. A few notes
    of condolence. Life continued on as if nothing had
happened. Prayers in choir, manual labor, adventurous

mission assignments for some, not like my domestic
    work of balancing the bank deposits for the priests'
work abroad. "*Should I stay or leave?*" Questions

skipping across seemingly serene meditations;
   at last *enlightenment* after a thunder storm:
as I heard an enchanting song of a dove on the deck

overlooking the Hudson valley. I *read into* this
   as a sign of *God calling* me back *to the world;*
my bag packed, I took the train south to the city,

subway to Brooklyn, borough of my beginnings.
   Statue of Liberty waving in the Bay. Next Easter
I'd go with my husband to see Lake Hopatcong again.

SANCTUARY
   for Joseph

Do you recall that August afternoon
   outside the city? An abandoned chapel,
where we dared do what the Rule forbid.
   Sunlight streaming through an opening
in the roof onto the dusty floor. Distant
   voices of villagers celebrating a wedding.
After months of separation, we couldn't get
   enough of each other's *real presence.* Valley
trembling with thunder. Bolts of lightning
   through the broken windows. Your damp
beard. Your heart's pulse. A rainbow arching
   over the clouds as you kissed the altar
stone. For a few hours we cuddled in the dark
   interior. Ashes of long ago incense stuck
to our clothes. We lit the tabernacle lamp
   as a sign of love's burning benediction.
Birds of paradise shuddered in a fading
   mural. A phoenix nurturing her young
at the exit. The flame tongued dove flew
   over your shoulders. We sipped red wine
in a silver chalice, enjoyed homemade bread.

96

MONT-SAINT-MICHEL

Following a lightning storm that tore across
the sea, we climb the slippery street to our B & B.
      Stars circling Saint-Michel's head. Sword poised,
wings unfurled. Ramparts icy cold. Galloping waves
      covering sand bars. Island refuge of Roland, Arthur,
knights, troubadours and ladies holding court. Proust
      set unforgettable love scenes not far up the coast.
Weather warms by midday, you're wearing short-
      sleeves. Golden hairs on your bare arms. Dark
scar across your knuckles. (Lawn mower accident
      in our Santa Clara California garden years ago.)
Healing takes time. *"Let's change our plans. Stay on."*
      Undertow of desire, wanting our vacation to
last longer. We celebrate Mass under Romanesque
      arches. Simple sanctuary windows. An abbot's
welcoming homily in several languages. Encouraging
      all to hug strangers at the *"Kiss of Peace."* Join
the community chanting: *"Ubi Caritas et amor, Deus
      ibi est."* Patches of moonlight cross our bedspread.
Dark blue sky sprinkled with stars. Brilliant Normandy
      coast. A chorus of humming waves. Salty seaweed
taste on our tongues. Cold winds whistle in the rafters.
      In the night heart and soul warmed by lovemaking.

AIX-EN-PROVENCE

A sycamore tree's golden leaves tumble towards
      the city's fountain fed by underground channels
built centuries ago by the Romans. I'm watching
      you walk across the avenue. August humidity
on your forehead. Cool drinks, a light lunch before
      we go our separate ways this afternoon. I'll visit

the local museum; you'll hike the hills overlooking
    Aix. We'll meet in our room by 5 to rest before
dinner. Trusting times apart, a rhythm we've practiced
    over the years, never foolproof against risk. Is there
such a thing as *too much freedom* in a relationship?
    Rilke's poem our inspiration-- lovers honoring each
other's need for solitude. (Yet Rilke refused to attend
    his daughter's wedding, claiming time to complete
his book. Did he practice in life what he preached in
    poetry?) If we're apart, for any length of time,
a magnet of longing draws us back, hugs, kisses,
    plus showers of forgiveness for any mistakes.

GERMANY 1938

No taking leave of our neighbors, since
    anyone might betray us to the police.
Quickly we stuff a few possessions into
    suitcases, fleeing our towns, villages,
cities under cover of darkness. No goodbyes
    at our grandparents' graves. Generation
after generation we've called this home.
    Our men risked their lives to defend
this land over centuries. We have served
    the community as teachers, doctors,
shopkeepers, lawyers, artisans, merchants,
    musicians. Now we're denied food,
shelter, jobs. Rounded up without warning.
    We wrap our babies in blankets, hold
our children's hands, sheltering our elders,
    as we hurry to the train, pretending calm,
praying that: *"Once across the border we'll be safe . . ."*

IRAQ, AFGHANISTAN

Aren't our American wars hidden from us at home?
Do we know how many men, women and children
    are maimed, killed in *our name: collateral damage,*
war on terror, national security. Soaring TV ratings for
    "reality shows." Celebrity, status, jackpots. *"Vote*
for your favorite performer! Twitter fast, faster! Post
    your latest *whatever* on *Facebook.* Personal details
matter. Meanwhile, if an insider reveals the wars'
    consequences-- *Beware!* what's happened to Bradley
Manning, the military whistle blower, whose still in
    jail. Even our traditional hero, Eisenhower, who
led *"the war to end all wars,"* warned in his farewell
    address: *"Be wary of the military-industrial complex."*

Some tout the Marshall Plan as proof of America's
    altruism. Yes, no, maybe, mixed motives, consider
John Le Carré's *Absolute Friends* unmasking U.S. wish
    to support a strong West Germany barrier up
against Soviet communist expansionism. So it goes,
    military bases spread across the globe, our latest
embassy in Iraq, the largest ever, set in the heart of
    Baghdad, a *Green Zone* apart from ordinary Iraqis,
while at home the faithful mantra's intoned: *"Best*
    country ever on the face of the earth!" "Hoist the flag!"
"Oh say can you see by the dawn's early light!" Can we
    see the rich getting richer, middle class collapsing,
poor growing poorer, our planet choking from CO2
    gases, politicians fighting over a deficit (fueled by
wars and a failure to raise taxes on the wealthy). And
    whatever you do, don't dare donate to *WikiLeaks,*
whose founder, Julian Assange (following Daniel
    Ellsberg's example) released government cables
suggesting war crimes committed by U.S. forces in
    Afghanistan and Iraq. *"How dare he discredit*

America's reputation abroad!" Do I, do you, do we
    dare to publicly protest for Manning or Assange's
freedom? Will I send this poem via the internet,
    risk our emails being classified as *suspicious.*
"Hush, brush unpleasant things under the rug."
    Recalling Freya Stark's history of the Roman
empire's defeat in their obsessive quest of outdoing
    Alexander who crossed the Tigris and Euphrates
into Persia (where he died in the desert) . . . exploits
    taking a toll at home: poverty, scarcity of food,
unemployment, homelessness; similarly the British
    (Germans, Dutch, Italians), now us Americans
caught in a perennial net of illusions, believing
    we're the best country, society, people ever
on the face of earth, our brand of *exceptionalism*
    pushing past limitations, seeking spheres of
influence over oil fields, trade routes, seaports,
    eliminating rulers we call dictators, so the cycle
spins out of control, stopped at the Persian border.

REIMS
    in memory of Natalie Budny

    "That's the young street and you are still just a child
Your mother dresses you in blue and white only / You are
    very pious and with the oldest of your comrades Rene Dalize
    You love nothing so much as the rituals of the Church."
    Guillaume Apollinaire *"Zone"*

Warm air of an August afternoon in Reims
Tapestries of Mary's Assumption line the church aisles
Champagne toasts at a restaurant facing the cathedral

Sweat on my forehead that I wipe with my hand
Someone who looks like Natalie waves and smiles
A breeze round my bare legs as I enter the vestibule

100

Back in Brooklyn the cool shadows of Holy Cross church
We pulled back the heavy drapes of the confessional
Wide doors swinging open to our Flatbush neighborhood

Flags flap crisply at trumpet blasting *"Alleluia! Alleluia!"*
A woman warrior named Joan crowns a prince of France
Outside a lush green lawn runs down the main road

Names of the WW I & II dead are inscribed in silver letters
My friend's innocence was natural unfeigned lovely
A unicorn in the tapestry raised his eyes and smiled at us

Chestnut trees offered shade during that hot summer day
Standing side by side the way we did at graduation:
"I'll never forget you." "And neither will I forget you."

The news of your passing arrived *out of the blue*
Your brother Robert's tender words in a letter
"You should have Natalie's rosary since you were best friends."

Years in different convents kept us apart
A continent separated us during our marriages
Is that you walking across the square

This August afternoon we're sipping champagne
Bubbles rising in our glasses tiny suns in pouring rain
Soon we're school girls again laughing as always

THE LAST SUPPER, MILAN

Finally we've found Leonardo's *Last Supper*
  on the refectory wall of a darkened 15th century
Milanese convent. Jesus has gathered his friends
  for a seemingly serene Seder. Sharing unleavened
bread, bitter herbs, wine. *"Why is he saying: "This is*

101

my body.   This is my blood offered for you." "Lose
your life and find it." "What does he mean? Has he
    forgotten the crowds waving palms as we came into
the city?" "Shouldn't this be our victory celebration?"
    "Does he doubt our devotion?" Storm clouds rumble
across the city. Lightning flashes in the doorway.

    My heart's beating fast. Is death near? Is Jesus
aware of his future sufferings? Are there signs of
    Judas's betrayal? Is Peter boasting and John
grieving? What happens after death? Will we meet
    around the corner at a train station, airport terminal,
cemetery, or the local park where we walked regularly?
    If the crocuses signal Spring and fresh green tips
press through the old growth redwoods, why not
    our resurrection too? I love the angel by Jesus'
tomb in the mural inside the church of my childhood.

    Such an engaging smile as he points to the doors
opening to Church and Flatbush Avenues, *the heart*
    of Brooklyn. Remember our loving through thick
and thin, rain or shine, *the whole kit & caboodle* of
    marriage, family, friends, work. Hand in hand,
turning towards the gate, the way it was when we
    left the convent and seminary on the other side
of the world. Carrying a poster of *The Last Supper*,
    we cross the piazza for a meal of Pasta Primavera,
fresh fish and red wine. Tomorrow's train to Ravenna,
    where Dante penned his reunion with Beatrice
in glorious circles of divine light, their *Paradiso.*

VALLEY OF OUR HEARTS' DELIGHT, SANTA CLARA

"First love, our love, filled with true devotion   .   .   ."
    lyrics lingering on a summer night at our
high school dances the year before I entered
    the convent. Embers of longing during

morning meditations preparing for your
      arrival. One December morning, a black
figure in the snowy fields coming to offer
      Mass at the convent. Soon we were sending
love letters delivered by a kindly priest, whose
      compassion sprung from his own loss, which
I witnessed, seeing him cry in the office (where I
      worked) after he lost the woman he loved,
since both their superiors forbid further contact
      between them, reassigning her far from him;
so, no doubt, he sympathized with our dilemma
      by carrying notes back and forth, thus allowing
our midnight calls, while the seminary and convent
      slept; I'd tip-toe to the kitchen pantry, place
Sister Ivan's chair as a barricade against the door,
      strike a match and dial your room. *"I've been*
waiting." "And I for you!" "What should we do?"
      "Let's leave." "Hold me close. Hold me tight.
It's you I've been longing for." Humming Elvis
      during our *exodus* to the land of almond orchards,
Santa Clara, California, *Valley of Hearts' Delight.*

AVEBURY, SAINT SARAH, SANTA CLARA

      An April sun breaks through fog brightening
the pebble path alongside the ledge lined by lavender,
      wild roses and heather, scenting the air, while we
descend a slippery slope to where grayish blue
      sarsen stones rise solidly in the damp declension
of green earth, shimmering with delicate turquoise
      lines swirling round their silvery circumferences.
Rain pockets mirror a bright sky streaked by shadows
      of birds in flight. Children are playing *Hide and Go*
Seek across the field. Suddenly you've vanished. I feign
      calm as I call your name, till you reappear round

the bend. *"Just wanted to see how fast you'd find me!"*
We hug as if we'll never let go. Wind whistles in
the woods. Tiny pools of light in rocky crevices. Pilgrim
	spirits seeking slivers of warmth after weeks of winter.
Bees humming in the clover, similarly at Saint Sarah's
	shrine as we descended stone steps beneath
the sanctuary and were surprised by a chorus of candles
	humming steadily inside that stone crypt reminder
of Easter Vigils in Santa Clara, California, holding candles
	with family and friends singing *Alleluias,* linked to
when we travel Route 17 from Santa Cruz to the Los
	Gatos rim, wind whistling through our hair, awestruck
by the beauty of the valley spread below in all her glory.

A MATCH MADE IN HEAVEN

A match made in heaven, so the song says. Her girlish
enthusiasm. His visionary charisma. Double dose of
foolish *bravado.* Tinder smoldering at first sight across
the convent's apple orchard. His brilliant mind. Her street
kid smarts. Both optimistically naïve by nature, pursuing
a spiritual friendship slipping into an overall passion, in
spite of pre-Vatican II's taboos with some rigid religious
rules forbidding getting together in twos, unless grated
official permission and not to talk at the wrong times
in undesignated places. They dared cast caution to
the wind, as others did too, in those *John XXIII* days,
making hay behind closed doors, a chair propped up
against intruders, spinning a cocoon of dreams together . . .

MONT-SAINT-MICHEL AGAIN

Fog filled side streets curve higher to our Norman
B & B. After settling in, we lean over the rampart,
watching high tide splash the island's fortified walls.
Monastic bells calling whoever wishes to chapel.

Concelebrating: *"This is my body. This is my blood."*
We often revive the ritual of entering and leaving
all for love. Wild white capped dark waves shimmer
in moonlight on high tides. Passionate kisses of peace,
desire, promising: *"I will be with you until the end
of time."* We're breathing close. Beads of sweat
on your forehead. Gentle brown eyes glow.
A fisherman carries nets over his shoulders.
I've stored your stories in my memory's alcove.
After celebrating Mass, we enjoyed a delicious
seafood dinner. Warming in bed, protective
shield of love, candles lit in the crypt carry our
concerns into eternity. Waters' leaping songs over
sandbars. *In manus tuas commendo spiritum meum* . . .

MAGDALENE'S CAVE, AIX-EN-PROVENCE

Centuries ago the Romans carved underground
channels through this region, so a fountain overflows
continuously into a moss covered seashell along
Boulevard Mirabeau, adding an artistic atmosphere
for locals and tourists, like us, who enjoy croissants
and dark coffee, wine and cheese before seeking
the legendary site of Magdalene's once-upon-a-time
cave in mountainous San Victorene. Twists and turns
up a narrow road, till finally we find her sarcophagus
covered by golden bees, signaling the Resurrection,
resembling Ravenna's Galla Placidia's honey hive
crypt of devotion to Empress Theodora echoing
Leonora's passionate aria pulsating in Verdi's
La Forza del Destino, when we were in standing room
at San Francisco's opera house, applauding another
curtain call, so we hummed on our way home; similarly
thrilling our collaborating on the Magdalene book,
as in recalling her shrine overlooking the Aix-en-Provence
hotel, a former convent, our room once a nun's cell.

No hard mattress, no pre-Vatican II rule forbidding
    particular friendships. A love nest blest by sachets
of lavender tucked under our pillows, chocolate-mints
    on the bedspread, the Mirabeau fountain bubbling
happily in the large scallop shell outside our window.

AFTERNOON OF A FAUN, VERSAILLES

    A summer sun bathes the blue basin. Poplars
wave lazily along the western horizon. Silvery
    fish splash our feet while circling Apollo's
golden chariot drawn by dolphins at the crack
    of dawn. A mischievous faun is winking
as he leans casually beside a bowl of miniature
    orange trees by the Grand Canal. Curly
golden hair sporting a crown of grape leaves.
    Green eyes glowing. Juicy wine stained lips.
Cloven feet stamping the earth as he plays
    a lively flute tune. An encircling family of
nymphs form a lively chorus. His downy fur
    shimmering in the breeze. I'm rubbing
the top folds of your ears, remnants of our
    animal ancestry. A nearby flock of tourists'
cameras are flashing. Suddenly the faun flees.
    Frightened nymphs follow. On rented
bicycles, we pedal fast as possible. Twigs
    cracking, branches catching our clothes.
Flute music fading in the underbrush. Silence.

AVEBURY AGAIN

turquoise threads   gray darkness   silent silvery chants

broken shards   rain pockets   ancestral ashes   *"Should old*

acquaintance be forgot . . ." guardian spirits   witnessing

106

world wars   sanctuary for peacemakers   sheltering exiles

comforting widows   children's playground   *"I depend on*

the kindness of strangers"   wanderers welcome   *"Be not*

afraid, I go before you"   *"I want you, I need you, I love you"*

gentle blue giants   angels of mercy   rain or shine   hot or

cold   Spring's first red-breasted robin   *"Hurry make a*

wish"   butterflies in heather   bumblebees in clover

"fourteen angels round about me"   oak trees humming

poplars too   I crown you with laurel leaves prince

charming   dove of peace   my darling dearest   dusty

honeybee   hearts aflame   imperfect beings   always

warts and all   northern lights   shooting stars   *"Sunrise,*

sunset, swiftly flow the years"   moon over our night's nest

April showers   caves concealing souls   windswept

plains   *"Look for the silver lining"*   healing rose hips

wheat sheaves   alfalfa sprouts   kale   chard   beets   nuts

a rainbow's spinning   sky kneeling down   kissing earth's

bounty   forgiving human failures   healing balms

encircling globe   reconciliation   even when things seem

hopeless   welcome home to all lost lambs   *"It's a far*

far better thing that I do than I have ever done before"   love

calls across the great divide   *"Hope springs eternal"*   hand

in hand   let's climb the hill   darkness and light dancing

SUMMER IN STRASBOURG

Arriving by train from Frankfurt, our first time in
France. An August evening in Strasbourg, we're
   sitting at a crowded outdoor cafe. Ripe tomatoes,
German pretzels, mild sausages, Kronenbourg beer
   after celebrating Solemn High Mass across the square.
A national holiday, feast day of Mary's Assumption.
   Amber lights in the cathedral's towers tonight. Bells
echo across Alsace-Lorraine. Wars fought by France
   and Germany over this region; now European Union
allies. This side of the Rhone is where Marie Antoinette
   first set foot outside Austria. I'm rambling in these lines
the way I will tomorrow wandering these side streets,
   since you'll attend the International Biblical conference
at the Hilton. Plane trees providing shelter along
   the river during breakfast. Dark roasted coffee and
an almond croissant. A couple strolls by, stopping
   to kiss passionately. I'm gazing at your open shirt
and hairy chest, your strong hands resting on the table,
   more than capable instruments of a keen intelligence,
builder of our Santa Cruz cabin, charismatic priest
   elevating the chalice, player of a fierce Scott Joplin
rag, shaping my body's contours on glorious occasions.
   A motorcycle speeds by with a gal holding tightly to

the guy. Life is filled with unexpected adventures.

What if I had accepted the grant for Culture & Religion
at the GTU, would I be giving a presentation today too?

It's more than okay that poetry became my calling.
Gratefulness goes a long way. Am I preaching to
    myself in this poem? Peruvian flute music fills
the square. You were a missionary for three years
    in Guatemala. I was missioned to count money
for the Maryknoll Fathers. Thank God we met at
    the Knoll. In Strasbourg we're laughing while
tossing aside the pink comforter. Rose glow of
    cathedral stones framed by the hotel window,
as we tumble happily into bed. Tomorrow Paris.

THE GRAND CANYON
for Joseph

Voices fading above the rim during the first thirty
    minutes of our six-hour descent into the baking
hot canyon. Red-tailed hawks glide by at eye level.
    We're slipping on the shale covered switchback
trail, stopping for swigs of water from the canteens
    crisscrossing our hearts. A hissing sound sets me
shouting: *"Rattle snakes! Run! Run!"* Your calm:
"It's okay, just crickets!" makes me laugh. At last
cool breezes rise off the Colorado River as we navigate
    the swaying footbridge. Shedding our clothes,
we wade into an icy clear inlet, splashing and kicking
    like kids. Floating on our backs, surrounded by
sunbaked benevolent cliffs. Light lingers in clouds.
    Soon we're snuggling in our cabin under a canopy
of stars. *"Are the boys okay at home?"* *"Don't worry.
I'm sure they're having a great time with grandma."*
Shimmering in your arms the way an aspen quivers
    beside our camp site. We wake before dawn.
Breakfast on the go, beginning our nine hour climb

along the twists and turns of the Kaibab trail.
Dust, dirt, stones, sand. Slow going in July's rising heat.
Stopping for our bag lunch on a deserted plateau--
"Oh No! A squirrel's stole my lunch!" Laughing we
share my peanut butter and jelly sandwich.
You urge me on, resuming our trek, silently sweating
in a temperature too intense for talking. I slip into
daydreaming of last night's bliss by the river. Canyon
creatures tumbling in the underbrush. Your joyful
announcement: *"We've reached the rim!"* A photo
shows our red faces beaming under straw hats,
arms round each other's waist, hiking sticks proudly
planted beside us, auburn shadows, silvery rapids
heading west, home to our California in the morning.

MYCELIUM
for Phyllis Koestenbaum

Shamans wrap embers of the home fires
within mycelium's protective coverings of
moss and lichen for careful transporting
of their smoldering treasure to new sites for
their people's survival; similarly how you
distill the essences of your history and heritage--
granddaughter of a Hebrew scholar, graduate
of Radcliffe, student of Yiddish, daughter of
an English professor, mother of four, devoted
to your original calling as shamanic poet, teacher,
truth teller, magical weaver of language,
down-to-earth wisdom, brilliant cultural insights,
ethical reasoning woven within relationships
of love, society, history simmering in stanzas,
groundbreaking lines, subtle wit igniting
profound reflections, sustaining your readers.

APPALACHIAN TRAIL, SHENANDOAH, POTOMAC
for Joseph

Oh Shenandoah! oh Potomac!   we love your roaring waters

beside our honeymoon hike   cataracts   falls   whirlpools

midnight silences   dragonflies   tadpoles   frogs   fish

rocks   reeds   maples   evergreens   beavers   butterflies

Oh Shenandoah! oh Potomac!   deep down sheltering glory

Chesapeake's Atlantic shores   we sign the hiking log

September heat wave   our trek across the Blue Ridge

mountains   ten miles a day   awed by owls   bears

moths   foxes   raccoons   deer   spiders   our shy new

lovemaking   enfolding each other's blissfulness

a warm *usness* quickly   slowly   gladly   flowing

our Alleluia oneness   cascading streams   upper falls

shorelines   crevices   ravines   cliffs   inlets   coves

abodes   humans   animals   vegetables   minerals

thunder   lightning   pines   aspens   birches   eagles

oh Shenandoah! oh Potomac!   we're whispering pet names,

falling asleep in each other's arms   darkness hugs dawn

dew bathes our green canvas pup tent as we crawl from

sleeping bags   butterflies shedding cocoons   we begin

again to climb ridges   descending ravines   scaling

boulders   exiting on a backcountry road   we face

a pack of barking dogs   I'm scared silly   you coach calm

"Hide fear, pretend bravery!"   I hitchhike us a ride   we're

holding tight   tossed about in the back of a pickup truck

we're laughing like kids   bales of hay itching our backs

at last Harper's Ferry   sheltering John Brown's final stand

our green VW bug's waiting   *oh Shenandoah! oh Potomac!*

bless us following instinct's call   flowing as one great waterfall

HOMAGE TO JOHN KEATS

If I were you, would I have chosen far-off Italy
As a last attempt to save my life and in doing so
Have to live apart from my heart's home   .   .   .

The Spanish Steps that summer drenched by a sudden
Thunder storm as we climbed towards those small rooms
Darkened by your death, yet lit within a single scene--

Your spirit soared above the space your bed occupied,
As though you left behind silvery lines we could climb
So find fields of glory fed with seeds of such brilliancy

Blooming in the soil of stanzas during a final winter's
Silence, though missing Spring round the corner, your
Courage crafted truth and beauty for poetry's future.

RENDEZVOUS, CROTON-ON-THE-HUDSON, NY
for Joseph

In the movie, soon after the couple arrive in
    Florence and reach their room at the hotel
across the Arno, they jump into bed, reminding
    me of those months, when I'd meet you at
Croton-on-the-Hudson, so you'd drive your
    trusty VW bug across Bear Mountain Bridge,
past Lake Tiorati through the Seven Lakes region
    for our hike far into the forest, your strong
hands hammering the tent's stakes into earth,
    green canvas rising for a few hours on Saturday
afternoons, till retracing our steps before sunset,
    we'd kiss goodbye, wave as the train hugged
the Hudson shore, I'd reach Grand Central station,
    take the IRT line to Foster Avenue, Flatbush--
laughing as I looked in the mirror, tiny wisps
    of sleeping-bag feathers stuck in my hair,
as I wondered if you found similar telltale
    signs of our lovemaking in your beard?

OUR BOYS, ONE SUMMER, VERSAILLES
for Eddie and Peter

Beside the Basin of Apollo, when the sun was high
overhead, we heard the voices of children calling
in the forest and realized it was our sons, who
disappeared on rented bicycles and we didn't
tell them the name of our hotel. Not that they
need to know, unless they get lost and ask

a stranger for help. Whatever, they have each
other to compare our casual directions: "*How
about seeing Trianon before lunch; down that pebbly path,
then turn left at the pond.*" What if we were wrong?
They've vanished between thick bushes and tall trees.
I began rushing, you were walking calmly, trusting
their instincts. I've always admired your mantra:
"*all will be well,*" while I'd practice pretending calm.
Yes, proud of our boys' independence, feeling safe
in France, though they don't know the language.
An opening far in the forest: "*There they are!*"
Eddie's running round the pink marble pillars
of Trianon. Peter's balancing on its low wall.
Chasing, calling, hiding behind bushes, playing
the way they do at home in our San Jose,
California neighborhood. Carefree, beautiful
boys, mischievously funny, best friends, brothers.
"*Hey, Mom, Dad, we're hungry! Let's meet at that
little cafe near the guy whose riding his chariot across
the water. Next time why not rent bikes like us!*"

FRANCIS

Brought up in a wealthy household, heir to his
    father's textile fortune, Francis inherited his
mother's compassion and love of Nature.
    One day, while walking in an olive grove,
he came upon a rustic cross and heard Christ's
    call: "*Give up everything and serve the poor.*"
So Francis shed his clothes, friends, and family.
    No more adventurous exploits as a soldier
riding horses in the countryside. He began
    begging for food, asking anyone he met for
help in serving the poor. His hands became
    worn from building shelters and a chapel

114

with a band of volunteers, whom he called
   brothers and sisters. All were welcome,
especially the homeless, the outcasts. Francis
   greeted lepers with a kiss, calling each:
*"my sister, my brother, my mother, my father,
   my friend, my child."* Authorities feared his
popularity. Was he fermenting a revolution?
   Why were young people joining his work,
refusing to fight in wars? Why were they
   choosing a life of poverty and service. Where
was this leading to? Letters of outrage were
   carried to the pope. *"Stop this fanatic who
is causing our young to leave their families for
   a life with the poor. We beg you, order this man
to obey you."* So in ragged clothes, Francis
   reached Rome by foot. Who knows what
was said between the pope and pauper; perhaps
   the aged man saw his earlier self in the young
one's idealism. No excommunication. No prison.
   No punishment. After all, this beggar was
harmless, living and working among the poorest.
   Not a crime and over time this fad of the young
following him will fade. They'll give up such
   hardships and head home for a comfortable
life. Francis died at age 48 before his beloved
   partner Clare. Today his shabby robe and worn
prayer beads are displayed in the enormous basilica
   built in his name on the cliff overlooking Assisi,
where frescoes by Giotto illustrate the saint's life,
   while the cross that Francis heard speak to him,
now smiles in an inconspicuous alcove within
   the Poor Clares' chapel down the street   .   .   .

DANTE, RAVENNA

Wasn't it October when we found him
   within the shadows of a chestnut grove,
   not far from the sanctuary of a Franciscan
church at the end of that cobblestone street,
   while the light was leaving and the guard
   was ready to lock the large brass door
of the tomb; the Vesper bells sent doves
   flying from the church tower across
   the Square as we stepped inside . . .
now I've returned alone, lost in daydreams,
   reading his long ago poem of following
   Virgil through Hell's scalding torments,
painful scenes of men and women swirling
   perpetually in their worse deeds, though
   thankfully Purgatory's penitents eventually
freed at the edge of eternity, so relieved of
   drought and despair, ah, Dante drank fully
   from his guide's understanding hands,
not becoming unglued, as can happen if
   not having a clue at which direction is
   best . . . where to go next . . . thankfully
I was led to the ancient texts of one who
   pursued love past loss, praying I'd be
   likewise blest by bliss, after passing
through fiery purifications, facing faults,
   foibles, sins of omission, mine and others,
   forgiving and being forgiven, rising within
a unifying field of glory, sky clear of clouds,
   dawn's benevolent beings, ancestral spirits
   singing, my beloved's waving from beyond . . .

VESTAL VIRGINS, THE FORUM, ROME

After battles, he'd arrive in Rome, parading
across the Forum, under the raised swords of
   soldiers, beneath the Arch of Titus, enjoying
the applause, shouts, salutes, the uproarious:
   "Hail Caesar!"-- while rumblings of rebellion
in the underground chambers of the nearby
   Vestal Virgins, who were forced to serve
the empire's goals for 30 years by tending
   an eternal flame, thus reassuring the Roman
population that good fortune would abound;
   though they'd be blamed for drought, lost
battles, pestilence, falling fortunes and suffer
   punishment if things turned badly; so it was
some sought refuge in the *Magnum Mater*,
   who tended them in sickness, encouraged
their dreams of freedom, equality, happiness,
   who played her harp for the women and girls
dancing on summer nights under the stars . . .

SALVADOR DALI'S PORTRAIT OF CHRIST

Dali's portrait of the naked man isn't bloody,
   but beautiful, though his face is hidden,
turned sideways. No visible wounds or
   nails holding him aloft, instead smooth
blocks of blond wood fasten Christ to the cross
   that is suspended in a clear blue sky, while
his beloved John stands below, recalling:
   "when you share a meal remember me, when
you care for the sick, the homeless, prisoners,
   the unemployed, the children, when you speak
truth to those in power, believe I'm beside you . . ."
   while I wonder what did Dali believe

or disbelieve about Christ. I believe, I doubt.
John composed his gospel during years of
exile on the island of Patmos. Believe it or not,
I feel shy revealing my beliefs publicly in poems.

ROSICRUCIAN MUSEUM GARDENS, SAN JOSE, CA

Last night's rain coats the amber obelisk's
hieroglyphics at the main entrance to San Jose's
Rosicrucian gardens. Mount Umunhum's visible
to the south, Mount Hamilton in the eastern
Diablo range, the dark green Santa Cruz mountains
rippling on the Pacific horizon   .   .   .

Our ritual starts at the small fountain flowing
into a dark blue tile basin shaded by an olive grove
before the path circles round redwoods leading to
feathery papyrus rows, before the scribe kneeling
at the temple door, as he pens a sacred text, while
you explain the papermaking process of peeling
open of bamboo type stems that are weighed down
to dry in the sun, then the writings are wrapped
layer by layer in containers to hide in the shade, as
was done in caves with the Dead Sea scrolls, that you
studied for your sacred scripture writing and teaching.

Acting as pilgrims, we approach our favorite
shrine to Iris, whose wearing an aquamarine robe,
welcoming all with open arms, as she balances
barefoot on a crescent moon guarded by four lions,
who pour water from their mouths into the sky
blue star shaped pool facing the sanctuary.

Legends say Isis was devastated after Osiris
vanished; so she searched the Nile and every corner
of the land for remnants, hints, clues, relics hiding

his whereabouts; similarly after Eros disappeared,
Psyche sought him continually till she collapsed
in failure, revived at the last minute by Eros's
healing kiss; and Magdalene discovering Christ
disguised as a gardener three days after he died,
though her *good news* was rejected by friends; only
convinced when they witnessed the clouds parting
40 days later as the flame tongue dove's descent;
ah lost, ah found, your smile and open arms after
you exit the plane, hugging hums at San Jose airport.

Leaving the garden, you'd draw me close
To the obelisk's hieroglyphics: Isis's long arms,
Osiris's open palms reaching for the sun, falcons
circling their heads, scarab beetle signifying renewal,
guardian lions warming their fur under rose and cross.

Neighborhood kids calling. Traffic humming
along Naglee Avenue, tourists visiting mummies,
not far from Mom's Calvary Methodist Church,
Mission Santa Clara, The Alameda, El Camino Real
and our home on Emory Street. You've passed over.
I linger in the olive grove. Black stains on amber
flagstones, as though tears leading to Isis's shrine.
Date palms swaying— *"valley of heart's delight."*
You often picked fruits that fell in the tall grass by
the curb. We'd head home through the municipal
Rose Garden, where our sons used to hop the fountain's
fence with friends fishing for coins in the light
blue pond reflecting a circle of redwoods.

A bouquet of miniature roses and a lavender candle
beside your photo. Jelly beans arranged by our grand-
child encircling a redwood burl. At dusk, if the clouds
dissolve in the darkening blue sky, a full moon may
appear through our window, light caressing your face.

119

EASTER

April in Ossining, New York, our sisters singing
The Lamentations of Jeremiah in choir. You appear
at the altar in a purple stole during the Holy Week
service. Three days later you're wearing a white
and gold chasuble. *Alleluia* sparks fly across the aisle.
Love-struck receiving communion from your hands,
formalizing our commitment at Saint Mark's chapel
in Greenwich Village, (a sanctuary for draft-dodgers),
soon sealing our covenant in Saint Patrick's Lady Chapel,
lots of kisses followed by two kids, *Hosannas* springing
above skyscrapers, carrying palms along Fifth Avenue.
Lilies line the path to Rockefeller center. Coconut cream
chocolate Easter eggs on our way to the 42nd St subway.

SUNDIAL, SANTA CLARA, CALIFORNIA
in memory of Joseph

Your gentle voice as you lead me round the sun-
    dial in the Mission cemetery across the street,
where you perform the ritual of tracing the sun's
    slim dark line circling the dial's center, while
joyful as a child, you announce the hour and
    minutes of the day, though I knew, without
saying so, your time was running out, as I was
    trying to discern how you wanted things at
the end . . . I trimmed your hair on the last day
    of your conscious life, grayish black strands
falling gently on the kitchen floor, as I was adoring
    your high forehead, sensitive mouth, intelligent
brown eyes, Roman nose, large listening ears. Wisps
    of silky hair held in my fingers. Your strong hands
resting patiently in your lap . . . Months later, I'm
    numb with loss, seeking for traces of your presence

120

wherever we have been, as when I finger the line of
   light turning round the dark sundial's center . . .

AVEBURY ADAGIO

silvery threads   darkened clouds   sun weakens north

sisterly sarsen stones   surrounding spirits   dearly

departed   *"Where are you now"*   we hiked these hills

circling burial mounds *"Stand beside me when the going gets*

rough" *"angels of God my guardians dear"* sentinels set

in earth   chorus of compassion   *"Be not afraid, I go before*

you" daffodil fields waving   heather filled hills   leaping

streams   healing hugs   gentle giants   nearby pub's

delicious pies   children singing   *"fourteen angels round*

about us"   butterflies in clover   bees in rosemary   fauns

in the gloaming   anything's possible   after all is said and

done   silvery monoliths hum   ancestral pathways offer

a waiting chalice *"Drink to me only with thine eyes and I will*

pledge thee mine"   darkness resurrects dawn's greeting

kids are heard rolling down the hill   Morris dancers spin

someone calls across the green *"Do you believe in spirits?"*

why not   anything is possible   sacramental signs smile

inside this stone circle as we gaze into each other's eyes

"How sweet thou art, how sweet thou art"   dearly departed

descending/ascending   *"Calling all angels"*   *"Look for the*

silver lining"   *"Somewhere over the rainbow"*   dark night

of the soul   *"Where are you hiding"*   I light two candles

beside your shrine   sew seams of your courage inside

my soul's tattered faith   *"Hope springs eternal in my heart"*

TRANSFIGURATION
in memory of Joseph

Hiking was a pastime you enjoyed, so why not turn to
    a new trail? I was watching your graceful stride,
    yet your hands were clenched as if possessing a secret.
Were you preparing to say goodbye, but didn't know how
    . . . we were walking along a country road, suddenly
    you turned towards Mount Tabor sparkling above us.
Sweating, stopping, starting again, we pressed on till
    reaching the top. Sunlight in your eyes was almost
    blinding. I fell back, or was it instinct, since the sky
lit up with lightning. Thunder rumbled in the rocks.
    Weren't we at risk atop the mountain? Your clothes
    seemed on fire. Did you rise off the earth, or was I
hallucinating? Shock waves of an earthquake under
    our feet. Did the parting clouds provide a ladder for
    ancestors descending or was I dreaming? Everything
grew quiet. Clouds thickened. Lightning ceased. We

hiked down, took the road leading into town, where
    others were expecting you. Looking back now, perhaps
I was being prepared for the time you'd pass over and
    I'd search in vain, struggling to believe we'll be reunited,
    so now recalling that day's transforming hike together.

ASHES AFTERWARDS, JOSEPH

. . . ashes afterwards contained in an alcove at home,
    your photo, a vase of flowers, miniature oranges,
your Maryknoll mission cross; I'm not ready to
    let go; recalling our lighting candles at the Black

Madonna's shrine in Chartres, or when we brought
    a bouquet for Heloise, Abelard and Proust's grave-
sites in Paris's Pere Lachaise, on to Balzac's home,
    where you translated aloud his love letter to

Ewelina Hanska that we found behind the door of
    his study; years later we strolled the damp decline
of earth inside Avebury's stone circle, the following
    week we climbed Mount Torn, our path blocked by

cattle, you laughed and kept on, while I, less brave,
    retreated to the car, everything charged by legends,
as at the golden pond suggestions of the Holy Grail
    and back in Glastonbury, the final resting place

of Guinevere and Arthur, side by side, their names
    inscribed in stone within what was once a magnificent
monastery's sanctuary, now a shell of its former self,
    lush green lawn blanketing the nave, blue sky peeking

through shattered Gothic arches; another time and place,
        your ancestral Italy, we were tourists tossing coins
overhead into the Trevi fountain near your Alma Mater,
        the Pontifical Biblical Institute, walking distance to

the Forum, where we were surprised by the Great
        Mother's shrine on the Palatine hills, perhaps
a forerunner of the Madonna, as the Baptist for Christ,
        also our pilgrimage to Keats's rooms overlooking

the Spanish Steps; years earlier, you picked me up
        at Croton-on-the-Hudson, we crossed the Hudson
in your red VW bug, past Bear Mountain, where we
        pitched a green tent in the forests by Lake Tiorati;

best of all our marrying at Saint Mark's rectory in
        Greenwich Village under a poster of Che Guevara,
we rented an attic in Brooklyn, ate Nathan's hot dogs
        in a saw-dust room at Coney Island, a short drive

to Our Lady of Refuge parish on Ocean Avenue,
        where my parents married, close to my childhood
parish of Holy Cross, while you grew up in New
        Rochelle, Westchester county, an Italian boy

attending Irish Iona Prep, then Manhattan College;
        a miracle, I believe, our meeting as Maryknollers,
leaving to marry, starting a family, migrating west
        with our sons, settling in the *valley of our hearts'*

delight, gathering with loved ones over years sharing
        meals, celebrating Christ's *Last Supper* call to pray
for Love's *real presence* felt throughout our lives, so I try
        follow your example as I call for you *dear Joseph!*

124

ADIOS, VAYA CON DIOS, JOSEPH

Sometimes I foolishly imagine a miracle bringing
   you back to life, or I daydream us again together
arriving at the doorway at Dante's tomb in Ravenna,
   close by the church of Saint Francis, where goldfish
were swimming in a pond under the sanctuary. Now
   home in California, I seek comfort and courage
to believe, as Dante did, in reunion with his beloved
   Beatrice and recall the morning train we took
to Venice, pilgrimage site across the Grand Canal,
   Titian's *Assumption of Mary* in Santa Maria
della Salute. Tiny angels were dancing round her,
   as she rose in glorious robes of red, blue and gold.
Have you ascended also? Once-upon-a-time you
   drove a U-Haul truck across the Great Divide,
over the Rockies and high Sierras, so preparing
   a home for us out west. I flew with our baby
boys, 747 from Milwaukee; you picked us up in
   San Francisco, grand reunion, driving down
to Santa Clara, our garden home of hearts' delight.

Notes on several poems:

I. BROOKLYN AND THE CATSKILLS

Mrs. Hanley, Prospect Park.   Mrs. Mary Hanley was a wonderful mother of eleven children. Her oldest, Judy Hanley (Mauro), was my first childhood friend.   Along with my grandmother Florence Skea Ball, I feel that Mary Hanley embodied *The Great Mother* archetype as described by psychologist Erich Neumann in his book by that name.

Holy Cross Church, Flatbush Brooklyn.   This was my childhood parish and school; Aileen Cleary and Natalie Budny were my close friends in grade school and throughout high school.

Silver Lake, Camp Oh-Neh-Tah. This camp in East Windham, New York, was founded by the Herald Tribune Fresh Air fund to offer two-week vacations for New York City girls.   Our camp director Miss Dot was a professor from an Ohio Women's College. She led us in gospel singing, traditional Protestant hymns and typical camp songs. Alongside a diverse cooperative community, I experienced the joys and challenges of living close to Nature. At age 14, I became a junior counselor after attending camp since age 10.

Survival Skills, Riis Park Beach. This public beach, near our Brooklyn apartment, is where my family enjoyed the Atlantic Ocean.   As a child I almost drowned in Lake Ronkonkoma, which is the largest, deepest lake on Long Island, a sacred site for Native Americans.

II. CONVENT

In this section I focus on my years as a Maryknoll sister, shortly before the liberal Vatican II council. These poems, along with those in my earlier collection *Transparencies,* were inspired by Maryknoll Sisters Mary Xavier, Paul Miriam, Ita Ford, Carol Piette, Maura Clark, Lil Mattingly, Mary Driscoll, Maris Stella, Mary Lou Andrews, Matilde, Delores Barbeau, and Eileen Mary.

Clare (1194-1253) and Francis of Assisi* (1181-1226)** and ***Clare's Prayer. I was influenced by Zeffirelli's film *Brother Sun, Sister Moon* and visiting Assisi with my husband Joseph Grassi.

III. TERESA OF AVILA, JUAN DE LA CRUZ

Teresa of Avila (1515-1582) *and **Juan de la Cruz*** (1542-1591) met for the first time at his ordination. In composing these fictional poems, I was influenced by Teresa of Avila's *Autobiography, Way of Perfection* and *The Interior Castle* along with Juan de la Cruz's *The Dark Night of the Soul.* Today the remains of Teresa of Avila and Juan de la Cruz are revered together in her Carmelite convent chapel in Avila.

IV. CALIFORNIA

Nearby Salem. I am indebted to Arthur Miller's play *The Crucible,* which I read as an undergraduate at CUNY-Brooklyn College, and Nathaniel Hawthorne's *The Scarlet Letter.* Our Maryknoll novitiate was located in Topsfield, Massachusetts, so we'd walk to the dentist in nearby Salem.

In Memory of Dr. Joseph Henderson. Dr. Henderson was a founding member of the C.G. Jung Institute of San Francisco. He authored many well-known psychology books. Among his patients, when he began his Jungian practice on the East Coast, was the painter Jackson Pollock.

Hopkins and Bridges. Forming the background for this poem is the poetry of Gerard Manley Hopkins S.J. (1844-1889) and his correspondence with his close friend Robert Bridges (1844-1930). While Bridges became poet laureate of England, Hopkins remained unknown in his lifetime. After the Hopkins died, Bridges helped publish his poetry.

Søren Kierkegaard. The Danish writer Kierkegaard (1813-1855) is considered to be the first existentialist philosopher. I am grateful to the late Professor Will Herberg (author of *Protestant, Catholic, Jew. . .)* for his Drew University graduate seminar: *The Problem of the Self in Western Thought,* and for his encouraging my presentation *Kierkegaard: the Self, the Single One, and the Crowd.* (At the time of this class, I was a young mother and my husband Joseph was teaching at Drew's Theological Seminary.)

Rilke's "Malte." This poem is based on my reading of several books about or by Rilke (1875-1926) (cf. *Rilke, A Life* by Wolfgang Lippmann and Robert Hass's Foreword to *Rilke's Selected Poems.)* Rilke's granddaughter was a Santa Clara University student in a poetry class taught by my friend, poet James Torrens SJ.

Reading James Merrill, Inverness, California. The poet James Merrill was a recipient of the Pulitzer Prize, National Book Award, Bollinger prize and other honors. Among his books are *The Changing Light at Sandover* and *A Scattering of Salts.* He was exceedingly generous to poets, including unknowns, such as myself. In 1989, I received an Ingram-Merrill Foundation writing grant. We corresponded during the last five years of his life. James Merrill died in 1995 from complications due to AIDS.

The Lawrence Tree, Taos, New Mexico. This poem is set at a ranch that Joseph and I visited outside of Taos, New Mexico, where   D.H. Lawrence (1885-1930) lived in a cabin beside a large pine tree. There he wrote *Saint Mawr* and *The Plumed Serpent*. (cf. *The Lawrence Tree* by Georgia O'Keeffe). Lawrence's ashes are buried in a chapel on this site.

Psyche and Eros, Inverness, California.   For this and other poems of mythic/psychological themes, I'm grateful for Jungian writer Erich Neumann's *Amor and Psyche* and his *Art and the Creative Unconscious*, plus Carl Jung's *Memories, Dreams and Reflections*. For imagining Eros's bouquet for Psyche, I was influenced by the *Bach Flower Remedies* (dilutions of flower materials for healing as developed by Dr. Edward Bach, a homeopath in the 1930's.) And *the wise friend* is psychologist, author, priest and professor Gerdenio (Sonny) Manuel SJ.

Heloise and Abelard. Peter Abelard (1079-1142) was a famed theologian and preacher, who fell in love with his pupil Heloise (1090-1164). As a punishment for this transgression, Abelard was physically mutilated and forbidden by his religious superiors to see Heloise. She entered a convent and became a beloved abbess. Abelard and Heloise continued corresponding. Seven hundred years after they died, their remains were reinterred side by side in Paris's Pere Lachaise cemetery. Joseph and I visited their grave site, where we met other *romantic pilgrims.*

The 99% (of writers). The brave actions of the protest movements across America are the inspiration for this poem. I believe elites exist within human organizations, whether medical, educational, political, financial, religious, cultural, social, personal. Too often unilateral, secretive decisions, made by an elitist minority, affect the lives of countless people.

129

Oh Tigris, Oh Euphrates. This poem, set in Iraq, was influenced by our U.S. wars in Iraq and Afghanistan, as well as by the political actions of Private Bradley Manning, WikiLeaks' Julian Assange, political activists Daniel Ellsberg, Daniel Berrigan SJ, the Plowshares movement, KPFA's radio programs as *Democracy in America, Letters and Politics, Mickey Huff's Project Censored,* and Freya Stark's: *Rome on the Euphrates, Dust in the Lion's Paw, The Minaret of Djam: An Excursion into Afghanistan.*

V. COLERIDGE

For my series of poems on *Coleridge* (1772-1834), I am grateful for the magnificent two volume *Coleridge Biography* by Richard Holmes, which includes details about the lives of William Wordsworth (1770-1850), and his sister Dorothy (1771-1855). Also, I drew upon Wordsworth's *The Prelude* and Coleridge's *Collective Poems and Letters.* When my husband Joseph and I vacationed in the Lake District, we toured Wordsworth's Dove Cottage, his Rydal Mount estate, and the childhood village of Dorothy and William. We hiked forest trails, lake shores, and landscapes familiar to Coleridge, William and Dorothy Wordsworth. I believe Coleridge loved Sara Hutchinson, and that for a time she reciprocated. After Sara chose to live in Wordsworth's household, since her sister Mary married William, Sara ended her relationship with Coleridge. I've fictionalized Dorothy's love for Coleridge.

VI. DONATELLO

Donatello's Christ. These poems refer to the bas-relief of *Christ with Angels* by Donatello, that my husband Joe and I came upon unexpectedly in London's Victoria & Albert Museum. Also, I recalled Donatello's sculptures that we viewed in Florence.

VII. SANCTUARY

Mont-Saint-Michel. Ever since the 8ᵗʰ century a Benedictine monastery has occupied the top of a small island called Mont-Saint-Michel off the French coast of Normandy. This site serves as a popular pilgrimage destination and tourist magnet. Joseph, I, and our sons vacationed on this island.

Magdalene's Cave, Aix-en-Provence. This poem draws on the legends that claim Mary Magdalene spent her final years in a cave above Aix. A chapel there serves pilgrims and tourists, who seek her resting place. It's possible that Verdi's portrayal of Leonora in his opera *La Forza del destino* was influenced by these Magdalene myths.

Reims. This city in the Champagne region of France is home to Notre Dame de Reims cathedral, where Joan of Arc crowned the Dauphin of France in 1429. While reading a Rimbaud poem about his childhood, I recalled vacationing in France with Joseph. Also I remembered my childhood friend the late Natalie Budny.

Valley of Our Hearts' Delight, Santa Clara. When the plum and almond orchards filled Santa Clara county California, it was called the *Valley of Heart's Delight.* Joseph, I, and our sons, Eddie and Peter, moved to the city and county of Santa Clara at the time it was becoming known as today's *Silicon Valley.*

Avebury, Saint Sarah, Santa Clara. Avebury, England, is the location for the largest stone circle in Europe, built of sarsen stones in 2,600 B.C. Druids consider it an *axis mundi* (center of the world) and gather there for rituals at the solstices and equinoxes. Saint Sarah's shrine, in the crypt of Saints Maries' church in southern France, is the sacred pilgrimage site for the Roma people. Joseph and I visited

Avebury, Saint Sarah's shrine and we often attended liturgies at Santa Clara University's church.

Afternoon of a Faun, Versailles. This is my playful attempt at a homage to Mallarmé (1842-1898) and his famed poem, *"Afternoon of a Faun,"* choreographed by Diaghilev (1872-1929) for Ballets Russes's virtuoso Vaslav Nijinsky (1890-1950). Also, I recall visiting Versailles and my attending San Francisco Ballet's performance of this marvelous work.

Mycelium. Often in traditional societies, before migrating, the shaman wraps embers of the home fires mycelium (mushrooms) as a sacred ritual to save the community's core flame. I believe Phyllis Koestenbaum is like a shaman in her practice of poetry. (Paul Stamets' book: *Mycelium Running* continues to influence me in his work and writing about the healing powers of mushrooms).

Appalachian Trail, Shenandoah, Potomac. During the years that my husband Joseph Grassi taught Sacred Scripture at Maryknoll seminary, he was an avid hiker and member of the Appalachian Trail group. After leaving religious life, we enjoyed a honeymoon hike along the Appalachian Trail (the section beginning and ending at Harper's Ferry.) The Shenandoah River flows from North Virginia through the Blue Ridge mountains to the Alleghenies and joins the Potomac River in a wonderful waterfall at Harper's Ferry, West Virginia. The Appalachian Trail is 2,160 miles from Maine to Georgia.

Homage to John Keats (1795-1821) refers to when Joseph and I visited the small apartment (now a museum) in Rome above the Spanish Steps, where Keats died. Also, on another vacation, we toured Keats' home at Hampstead Heath. I was also influenced by *John Keats' Collected Poems* and by Helen Vendler's *The Odes of John Keats*.

Rendezvous, Croton-on-the-Hudson, New York. Lake Tiorati is within the Seven Lakes of Harriman State park, New York, where my brother John attended Camp Sebago, and our brother Richard and his wife Loretta live and raised their family in nearby Sloatsburg, NY. Joseph and I used to hike this area near the Hudson River.

Francis / Dante / Vestal Virgins, The Forum, Rome / Dali's Portrait of Christ . . . these poems were added while I was reviewing proofs for this book. Also, I recalled Robert Bly's words years ago at a San Jose reading: *"No need to understand a poem, or like all of it; if one or two lines speak to you, then your coming tonight was worth-while."*

Rosicrucian Museum Gardens, San Jose, California. This museum has the largest collection of Egyptian artifacts in the Western U.S. Joseph and I raised our sons Eddie and Peter in San Jose's Rose Garden neighborhood, near this museum.

Acknowledgements Several of these poems were or will be published in the following: *America Magazine* (NY), *Caesura* (Poetry Center San Jose, CA), *Full Circle* (Maryknoll Sisters, New York), *The Montserrat Review* (San Jose, CA), *Psychological Perspectives Jung Institute* (Los Angeles)

**I rededicate this 2022 edition of Heart and Soul
to my late beloved husband Joseph Grassi**

Joseph A. Grassi was a renowned Sacred Scripture scholar, priest, author, social activist, and teacher at Maryknoll Seminary, Drew University, Marquette University and many years at Santa Clara University. For three years Joseph served the people of Huehuetenango, Guatemala, ministering to their spiritual, social and physical needs. His homilies were in Spanish or the Mam dialect, since he put together the first dictionary of that language. Besides his Biblical classes, Joseph studied and taught women's liberation, personal growth, simple living, meditation, healing heart imagery and Sufi dancing. Joe believed *"children are our best teachers,"* and he was a devoted father and grandfather, and the best possible love-partner on life's journey. Joseph and Carolyn Grassi co-taught Spirituality & Aging, Nature, Scripture & the Arts for the Osher Lifelong Institute at Santa Clara University.

Books by Joseph A. Grassi

Mary Magdalene and the Women in Jesus' Life (with Carolyn Grassi) (Sheed and Ward) // The Secret of Paul the Apostle (Orbis Books) // Underground Christians in the Earliest Church (Diakonia Press) // The Hidden Heroines of the Gospels (Liturgical Press) // Mary: Mother and Disciple (poems by Carolyn Grassi) (M. Glazier) // Changing the World Within, Personal and Spiritual Growth (Paulist) //
Children's Liberation: A Biblical Perspective (Liturgical Press) // The Secret Identity of the Beloved Disciple (Paulist Press) //
The Five Wounds of Jesus and Personal Transformation (Alba House) // Informing the Future: Social Justice and the New Testament (Paulist) // Jesus Is Shalom: A Vision of Peace (Paulist) God Makes Me Laugh (WIPF & Stock publishers) //
Broken Bread and Broken Bodies (World Hunger) (Orbis Books) Healing the Heart, Transformational Power of Biblical Heart Imagery (Paulist reissued by: Wipf and Stock Publishers, Oregon)

Book Cover Writers' Credits

John Ashbery, world-renowned poet, and author of more than 30 books of poetry, including the acclaimed *Self-Portrait in a Convex Mirror*, recipient of the Pulitzer Prize, National Book Critics Circle Award and many other literary awards.

Grace Cavalieri, producer/host of *The Poet and the Poem from the Library of Congress*, author of many books of poetry, producer of plays and operas, recipient of the Folger Shakespeare Library Poetry's Columbia Award, the Pen-Syndicated Fiction Award, Public Broadcasting: Silver Medal and other awards.

Jack Foley, popular radio poetry host of KPFA: *Cover To Cover*, award winning poet, literary critic and author of several books of poetry and criticism, as his *Visions and Affiliations, California Literary Time Line, Poets and Poetry, volumes 1 and 2*.

Ron Hansen, is known for his fine short stories and novels include *Desperadoes, The Assassination of Jesse James by the Coward Robert Ford* (made into a Hollywood film), *Mariette in Ecstasy, Exile* (Gerard Manley Hopkins), *Atticus*, as a finalist for the National Book Award, *Hitler's Niece* and his most recent book: *She Loves Me Not: New and Selected Stories*.

Naomi Ruth Lowinsky, is a poet, Jungian analyst, literary critic and creative writing teacher. She is the author of *The Sister from Below, Adagio & Lamentation* and other volumes of poetry.

Paul Mariani, author of several books of poetry, and the award-winning biographer of *Robert Lowell, Gerard Manley Hopkins, William Carlos Williams, Hart Crane, John Berryman*.

A.David Moody, poet and renowned literary critic, author of *T.S. Eliot, Poet*, biographer of *Ezra Pound (Vol I and II)*, is co-editor of *Ezra Pound To His Parents, Letters 1895-1929*.

PREVIEW: ITALIAN POEMS BY CAROLYN GRASSI
(to be published by Patmos Press San Francisco)

FRANCIS OF ASSISI
in memory of Joseph

Olive trees and mustard fields dot the Umbrian
    valley. You're retracing those years you sought
the saint you loved when you were a young man
    inspired by Francis's poverty of spirit. A semi-
lit alcove in the basilica's crypt displays the saint's
    hair-shirt, robe, rosary and sandals. Giotto's
frescoes of Francis's life cover the main nave's ceiling.
    We find the miraculous cross of Christ at a small
altar of the Poor Clares' convent down the road. We meet
    a novice who paces San Damiano's cloister. At age 18
you left your New Rochelle home and entered Maryknoll
    seminary. After ordination, you were sent to
study Sacred Scripture for three years in Rome. Often on
    weekends and vacations you hiked the countryside,
ministering to the poor in rural parishes, plus several
    pilgrimages to Assisi. Legends say Francis left
his father's home and never returned, except as
    a beggar. You turned away from your father's
construction company. Your wanting what he
    did not want, a life among the poor, his having
left Italy at age 12 to work with his brothers in
    New York, as a way to support their family.
Statues of Francis's parents stand beside what
    was once their home. They're looking down

the road, hoping their son returns. Tourists are
    everywhere today. Francis is famous. Maybe
his father felt by publicly disowning his son that
    the boy would feel guilty and comply with his
family's wishes. His mother knew better, as did
    your mother, realizing that nothing would
dissuade your determination to become a priest,
    so she secretly wrote the rector of the seminary,
to overrule your father's *No*. Soon afterwards,
    your mother died, so your father gave permission
for your entering the seminary, honoring your
    mother's last wish. You've taught Maryknoll
missioners, served the poor in Guatemala for 3 years,
    then left religious life for another *calling*. Returning
as a pilgrim to Assisi, this time with me, your wife.

THE BRIDGE OF SIGHS, VENICE

Lifting its heart to the sky, the sea sighs. Light
mingles with darkness. Gondoliers are serenading
tourists: *O Sole Mio*. Through a tiny window of

the covered bridge a last look at freedom. Narrow
corridors and stark cells. Trap doors concealing
the Inquisitional Hall. Who tightened the chains?

Who betrayed whom? Who defended the accused?
Who offered comfort? Who visited the imprisoned?
Thunder cracks lightning's whip forcing confessions

from the brave and timid alike. Rain is pouring
through gargoyles' grimaces. Secret trials. Guilt's
a far gone conclusion. Nowadays America's prisons

overflow, even jails in progressive California. Alcatraz
glows through fog in San Francisco Bay. Once a prison,
now a popular tourist destination (similarly the Dodge's

Palace). Driving north across Golden Gate Bridge, nearby
San Quentin prison of purgatorial fires turning into hell:
In for decades or life, inmates endure a slow going torture.

consider *Amnesty International, the Red Cross* and *Red
Crescent* denouncing U.S. Guantanamo prison. Ah,
. . . bolts of lightning break through clouds across

the Grand Canal. Articles of torture clearly on display--
manacles, the rack, spikes, chains. Frightful feats
happened here. Are we Americans always blameless

abroad? Our drones, counter-insurgency attacks, collateral
damage: killing innocent bystanders. While back home
inmates are frequently incarcerated at prisons

far from their families. Yet the boasting blares non-stop:
We're the best country ever on earth! Such hubris flies in
the face of our so-called noble enterprises since we send

non-stop billions to arm countries fighting our proxy wars!
Why not funnel funds of reparations to the descendants of
slaves on U.S. shores? May peace prevail *Pacem in Terris* . .
.

PREVIEW: TANKAS BY CAROLYN GRASSI
(to be published by Patmos Press San Francisco)

280, Palo Alto, California

Mustard flowers and daffodils ripple inside the vast
property line of Stanford University, where cows graze
    in Spring grasses, as I join the commuter traffic
heading south on 280 towards the congested suburbs
of what was the once-upon-a-time lush Santa Clara valley.

A PATCHWORK QUILT, SAN FRANCISCO BAY

Pacific tides push and pull sailboats past
Golden Gate Bridge and spin windsurfers as
    tour boats circle Alcatraz. Fog horns guide
freighters from China into Oakland's harbor.
Light beams from the hills of Berkeley homes.

WHAT IF MARX

What if Marx believed the only way to
assist the poor and oppressed was by social
    activism? What would the world be then
if he hadn't spent his life writing *Kapital* and
collaborating with Engels on the *Manifesto*?

C.O. STATUS

"Is this a just war?" she asked her son, who
shrugged his shoulders and enlisted anyway in
    the Army. She feared for his safety. Too late.
Soon he's deployed to Iraq. She feels like a failure
in not having raised him as a *conscientious objector*.

JOSEPH A. GRASSI

As a Maryknoller in Guatemala, you rode
a donkey into the mountains, slept on dirt floors
    with your people, healed children with sulfur,
pulled teeth, set up a clinic, created a dictionary of
their Mam language, bowed with them before the sun.

DEVOTION, ALBATROSS FATHER

Heavily weighed down with fish from Hawaii,
the albatross locks his wings, then coasting for
    miles and miles over the Pacific Ocean, to
bring home the only food his chicks can eat as
they wait with their mother in southern California.

BALZAC'S *EUGÉNIE GRANDET*

She fell in love with the young man, who
kissed her in the family garden, promising
    to return. Soon he married a wealthy woman
in Paris, forgetting Eugenie forever. She never lost
hope in love, spending her life in serving the poor.

KIERKEGAARD

Close to despair after breaking your
engagement to Regina, you became a recluse
    imposing penances on yourself, living
in solitude, devoting your days and nights to
God, whom you sought passionately in prose.

OVID'S EXILE

Rome's poet laureate was banished to the other
side of the world and pleaded to his former friend,
    the emperor, for a pardon. No reply. Simply
silence. So Ovid sustained himself by writing
love poems to his wife for the rest of his life.

MY MOTHER'S ECUMENICAL EXAMPLE

Raised in Brooklyn as an Episcopalian, Mom
converted to Catholicism along with her parents;
    as a Californian, she attended San Jose's Calvary
Methodist church, occasionally Mission Santa Clara,
or worshiped across the street at Church of the Valley.

JAPANESE KEY CHAIN
for Joanne Landers

Your gift of this medallion, a Kyoto woman
in a blue kimono on my key chain is a daily
    reminder of your kind ways, as when you
traveled a great distance to visit me one Fall,
long ago, offering courage at a time of crisis.

REDWOODS MONASTERY, WHITETHORN, CA
for Sister Veronique

My retreat's ended. We hug goodbye at
the monastery gate. Hazy wood smoke the closer
    I come to Garberville. South on 101 to congested
Bay Area suburbs. All year long I'll miss singing
with you in choir and our walks among the redwoods.

141

FACING FEARS
for Jerry Motto

As a U.S. soldier, staying overnight in a cellar
before the Battle of the Bulge, you read these words
    in stone over the fireplace: *"Fear knocks. Faith opens
the door. No one is there."* You became a psychiatrist
guiding patients with courage in facing their fears.

YOUR PHONE CALL
for Mary Jeanne Oliva

Pink, yellow, red and purple crocuses
peek through the dark damp earth, harbingers
    of Spring, brightening a cool Pacific coast day,
as your phone call this afternoon, your warm voice
carrying the sunshine of Santa Clara into my heart.

MEETING AGAIN
for Joseph Grassi & Tennant Wright SJ

Poinsettias brighten Santa Clara's mission
gardens under a bright blue sky. You pour green
    tea into three amber cups, serve rice cakes on
a yellow plate in your adobe room, sharing Zen poetry,
laughter, koans, such joy: you're back from Belize.

JAPANESE GARDEN, GOLDEN GATE PARK

Slightly hidden by thousands of plum blossoms,
an ant is seen carrying a crumb to Buddha's smiling
    lips. A lotus springs from the nearby muddy
pond. Bamboo stalks bend in Pacific breezes. Bees
humming in the roses. Pollen dust in the sage's palm.

VERSAILLES
in memory of Joseph Grassi

Clouds are vanishing over the forest. Gold
fish are hugging Neptune's bronze feet. Nymphs
splashing his beard. Breezes stir the bride's
silk dress as the groom holds her close under
the willow. Two hearts as one longing for night.

DEDICATION

Since *Heart and Soul Poems* was first published in 2014 several loved ones have passed over. I am keeping the dedication with renewed gratitude to my beloved husband Joseph Grassi, our sons, Eddie (daughter-in-law Alisa) and Peter, our grandchildren, Madeline and Ethan. I am grateful for the encouragement of my brothers, Richard (and Loretta), John (and Karen) Cook, and their families.

Thanks to Carol Connolly, Penelope Dinsmore, Diane Dreher, Julia Franco, Kathleen & Eric Hanson, Phyllis Koestenbaum, Barbara Hanley Koch, Judy Hanley Mauro, Dr. Efrem Korngold, Joanne & John Landers, Dr. Ferol Larsen, Pushpa MacFarlane, Patricia Machmiller, Ilse & Dan Meyer, Betty & Peter Michelozzi, Nancy Newman, Dorothy Nissen, Mary Jeanne Oliva & Stephen Estes, Theresa Schuman, Mary Lou Taylor, Sr. Veronique of Trappistine Redwoods Monastery Whitethorn CA, plus Maryknoll friends: Sr. Mary Lou Andrews, Beth & Tom Bastasch, Sr. Nancy Connor, Sr. Paul Miriam, Marita & Jerry Grudzen, Mary Heffron & Tom Fenton, Delia McGrath, Linda Montano, Pat & Jerry Motto, Karen Peterlin, Rosalie & Greg Rienzo, Katherine & Tom Samway, Terry Sissons, Betty & Jim Steidel, Mary & Jim O'Connor.

Gracias to Jesuit friends, Gerdenio Sonny Manuel S.J., Steve Privett S.J., Fred Tollini S.J., James Torrens S.J., and Tennant Wright S.J. Many thanks to my Camadolese community of Oblates led by Jacqueline Chew (New Camaldoli Big Sur, CA and Incarnation Monastery, Berkeley, CA.) and to the SF Jung Insitute, the Analytical Psychology Club of SF members/friends: Carole Dietrich, Jana Hutchinson, Judith Loveless, Stevem Frus, Helen Mendenhall, Ann Withers.

Special thanks to Ron Hansen for editorial advice and his Foreword, to Johanna Baruch for her beautiful painting *Wisdom and Innocence* that graces this book's cover, and to Mary Jeanne Olivia for her assistance in this 2022 edition.

My thanks to fine poet James Torrens S.J. for proof-reading, though any errors are entirely mine; thanks to poets/ mentors, who inspired and helped me: Robert Bly, Naomi Clark, Harry Ford, Robert Hass, Galway Kinnell, Louis L. Martz, James Merrill, A.David Moody.

I am grateful to mentors/teachers at Maryknoll Sisters College, Brooklyn College CUNY (B.A. in Political Science and Education), Drew University, Marquette University, and to San Jose State University (M.A. Political Science and M.P.A.) with gratefulness to Professors William McCraw, John Wettergreen, plus archivist Craig Simpson (of SJSU)

A bow of thanks to Poetry Center San Jose, California and its founder, Naomi Clark, who believed in my work at the beginning and generously helped me in countless ways.

Addenda to 2022 edition of *Heart and Soul*:
Excerpt: Carol Connolly Letter to Carolyn Grassi 2014

It's the evening of our visit and I have been reading your poems. After having gotten halfway through your book, I am immersed in the beauty of your language, your tenderness, sensitivity, and your loving spirit. These are beautiful poems! I am especially moved by those poems depicting your personal life of love and family. Truly, I have been moved to tears by some, especially those written about your life in California. I do think that these poems in Heart and Soul are the very best you have ever written.

(Note:. I met Carol Connolly in 1984, when we were ushers at the San Francisco Opera House. She died in March 2021. Carol would want me to share her letter, and so I dare to do that in her honor with immense gratitude for such a loving friendship. Rest in Peace, dear one.)